WEAVE

WEAVE

DEIRDRE SULLIVAN

First published in 2022 by Skein Press
www.skeinpress.com

Cover design and layout by Éilís Murphy of Folded Leaf
Illustrations by Yingge Xu of The Art of the Brush
Printed by Walsh Colour Print, Co. Kerry, Ireland

A CIP catalogue for this title is available from the British Library.

ISBN 978-1-9164935-7-5

Skein Press gratefully acknowledges the financial support it receives from the
Arts Council of Ireland.

Skein Press are also grateful to Dublin UNESCO City of Literature and Dublin
City Council for their support.

For Brian Keary – a candle in the window

CONTENTS

The seasons swirl one into the other, and often we have a foot in each. Imbolg is traditionally the time when the new lambs are born. The date isn't fixed; you have to watch and wait. A city dweller, I find myself looking for the snowdrops bursting through dark earth, and waiting for days to lengthen. The hunger for light and the sense of anticipation and liminality, as well as folklore about night-time encounters with the Other Crowd, inspired me as I worked on this story about unexpected connections, transitions and that strange twilight space where the world has stopped and anything seems possible.

———

The streetlights cast a golden glow on the footpath that promised morning, but not yet, not yet. Muireann flinched at the briskness of night air hitting her face, her two bare legs. She hadn't really registered the warmth of the club when they were in it, just the constant noise, the smell of people. Her fingers were sticky with the remnants of Natalie's sambuca. She'd spilled her shot and they had tried to wipe it up with beer mats, which didn't really work. They hadn't even been that drunk, not really. The rules were different at night. You could just say things, do things. Muireann wove her way through shoulders, cigarette smoke, after Joan.

It had been Shannon's birthday celebration, and she'd gone off in a taxi with Natalie and Oisín and Megan and Clodagh and Pól. Muireann had been left behind with Joan, who was a mess. One of the upstairs barmen was Joan's brother's friend Aidan, the one she fancied, and she kept going up there, ordering drink after drink and trying to talk to him and touch his hand. Natalie had rolled her eyes at Joan, like she was being pathetic, which she was.

Clodagh had pulled at them and said, 'Ignore her.' But Muireann had hung back, unsure what to do, and Joan had noticed.

'It's okay.' She'd winked. 'I'm not a nun. I know what I am doing.'

To be honest, though, she really didn't. Her bra straps had been poking out, and Muireann didn't think it was deliberate. She had this awful sense of disarray, of something just about to fall apart. There was a difference between thinking you were safe and actually being safe. She'd gone into the bathroom and splashed a little water on her temples, and when she had returned, Joan had been holding a little tray of shots while Aidan's face flickered with something between discomfort and politeness. Muireann wasn't a nun either, if that was what Joan had meant. She wasn't frigid. People sometimes called her that, though, because she didn't like it when they got all detailed about sex stuff. It wasn't that she wasn't curious, but the knowledge of how other people did it put a layer of something on her body that even by herself she couldn't shake. The things she was supposed to do, supposed to feel, *what other people did . . .* it made it into sort of . . . an assessment. Closed her up, and off. She didn't like that. She blinked her eyes and scratched her collarbone.

Joan was sitting on the windowsill of the hairdressers beside Boots. Across the way in the River Island doorway, Muireann could see the huddled form of a person sleeping rough while she was there brushing her friend's hair back from her face and wondering whether to go for chips or a cab home. It felt disjointed, like there was something off about the world, or more than one world happening at once.

The person's shoulder moved, as though they were trying to get comfortable, and Muireann had a sense that she was intruding on a private thing. She didn't know if she should look away, stop caring. She was almost grateful when Joan began to dry-heave into the purple beanie Natalie had given her for Christmas. Muireann didn't even think Joan was that nauseous, more bet on proving a point about whose job it was to do the minding. A glistening strand of spit curled in the corner of her mouth. She wiped it away with the heel of her hand and handed the beanie back to Muireann with a flourish. Her lipstick wasn't smudged, which was frankly incredible. The little white-gold ring her dad had bought her for their graduation caught the light. 'The cheap stuff always irritates my skin,' she had told Muireann once, brushing her fingers, light as cobwebs, over a little choker Muireann loved but hadn't worn since. 'I wish that I could wear something like that.'

Muireann emptied out the hat and folded it into the pocket of her jacket, knowing that from now on it would always be the hat that Joan had spat in. She didn't even seem to register what she had done, and was on her phone, angrily looking at Clodagh's stories. Muireann sighed. She didn't have the bandwidth. She placed a hand on Joan's shoulder and asked her if she wanted to get a cab or go for chips.

'Chips.' Joan smiled. 'Always, always chips. Drunk chips don't count. Was I okay with Aidan?'

'Yeah,' Muireann told her. 'You were fine. Sure, he only saw you at the bar, so, like, short interactions.'

'Yeah,' said Joan, but she didn't sound so sure of that. Her eyes looked out, beyond the cobblestones as though there were a fresh horizon there. Her voice was gentle: 'Can I please stay over?'

The question hung suspended in the air until Muireann eventually nodded. She couldn't think of a good way to say no. Joan could be touchy and had a talent for remembering slights. When she'd had the falling out with Clodagh, the sheer amount of stuff she'd brought up to support her argument. Messages left on read, rounds not gotten, taxis not paid for, an earring left in the dishwasher, and a refusal to pay for the repairman because it could have been anyone's earring – when Joan had three screenshots from her stories of Clodagh wearing that exact pair (which she had borrowed from Natalie, who didn't want to get involved). Joan, Clodagh never tired of saying, didn't even live in the house with them, so it was literally none of her business.

'Me and Clodagh are fine now,' Joan murmured, as if she could read Muireann's mind. 'We're fine now.' She didn't sound like she believed herself.

'I know you are,' Muireann said, placing an awkward hand on Joan's elbow,

'Come on, we'll go to Shakes.'

Shakes was a chipper that had been new and cool when they were fifteen but already looked a little dated. Peeling wallpaper with parrots on it. Neon palm trees.

'Do you think my drink got spiked?' Joan asked. 'I'm very wobbly.'

'No, love,' Muireann said. 'I think you just had more drinks than you normally would because you were enjoying chatting to Aidan so much.'

Joan's expression changed. She ran her fingers through her hair to fix it, and Muireann caught the gleaming ring again, imagined it catching her cheekbone, drawing blood. Not that Joan would ever do anything like that – she wanted to be a chartered accountant, for fuck's sake – but there was something about this strange space between night and morning, where things seemed possible, for good and bad. Joan's voice was low, but it cut through the air.

'Do you mean I was, like, being desperate?'

Muireann shook her head. 'Not desperate, no.'

She really hoped that Joan would let this go – she had been really into debating when they were in school and when she got an idea in her head after a few drinks, she could be like a dog with a bone. Muireann looked at the throng of people, elbowing each other to get their orders in. She swallowed, smiled.

'I'll go up for food. What would you like?'

Joan's eyebrows were knitted, and Muireann could tell that she was mulling over what had happened with Aidan, and blaming Muireann for mentioning it.

'Curry chips,' she said, perching haughtily against one of the bright pink bins and taking out her phone. Her eyes flicked down, and Muireann was dismissed.

She was going to get garlic cheese chips, she decided. She wasn't going to get with anyone at this stage of the night. There were a fair few guys in the queue, but she didn't make eye contact. Three a.m. chipper boys were a poisoned chalice.

She'd scrolled through the apps earlier, just in case, but nothing really. She was messaging a guy called Ed, but he never wanted to meet up. Just asked her things. Not even flirty things. Weird stuff, like if you were a dog what dog you'd be and do you ever think about Fat Bear Week. He felt more like a way to kill the time than a real, warm person she could touch. She probably wouldn't even recognise him if she saw him walking down the street. People looked so different in motion, and she had never been that good with faces. When she was in primary school they'd grown avocados from pits, and she remembered staring at hers, waiting and wishing and hoping it would grow. And when it did, it was just like any other plant. That curl of green. It was the in between time when it called to her. And maybe that was the appeal of Ed, he was a little seed. A question mark. Muireann felt a hand on the small of her back, and she startled.

'Get me a Diet Coke as well,' Joan said. There was a pause. She added, 'Please,' before returning to the bin.

Muireann ordered and waited at the counter. There was a guy beside her in a khaki shirt, which was a choice. His shoulders hunched, he was a little smaller than the others, wasn't with them. He was wearing brown Converse, and his cheeks were flushed with drink. He looked at her and nodded. She avoided eye contact but made her lips curve up in case he'd think she was a bitch and start to shout at her. You never knew with people. They could turn.

Joan had moved to allow people to get rid of their rubbish. She was near the door, her back to Muireann. Her curls were going limp but she stood defiant, daring the world to annoy her more than it already had. Muireann grabbed the big brown paper bag, the drinks, and walked towards her. She felt the eyes of him against her, and her skin felt tingly, on alert, as though he could see through her coat to the backless dress she'd worn to the club. It had been her sister's, a beaded twenties thing, but she had stolen it. Fionnuala was in New Zealand now; she wasn't coming back for it anytime soon. She pulled Joan by the hand towards the road. The house was a forty-minute walk away. And she could feel the horrors closing in. The curve of Joan's neck above her scarf. Chewing gum on pavement. Golden light. A cobweb stretched across the wing mirror of a car, glistening with dew. It was a work of art. It was a trap.

'My feet hurt,' Joan pulled one heel off, wiggled her toes and jammed it on again. 'This is going to take ages.'

'If you want to pay for the taxi, we can get a taxi,' Muireann said. 'I've nothing left till payday now.'

'You shouldn't have come out if you'd no money.' Joan's voice was whiny, as though Muireann's money troubles existed solely to annoy her.

'Sure, if I waited to be rich, I'd never do anything.' Muireann smiled. Her dad wasn't a vet and she didn't live in a five-bedroom house in close proximity to a riding school. Joan couldn't help her privilege, and Muireann shouldn't let it piss her off. Although it did. Joan made a sound of chip appreciation. Muireann smiled again, a little differently.

They walked along by the canal in silence. Chewing. Muireann pointed out a lone swan, neck curled in on its body, nesting.

'It looks like a big soft sleeping egg,' she said, and Joan nodded, a little sadly. Her hair was in her face again.

They leaned on the railings and looked at it. Muireann's feet hurt too. The balls of them. A sort of meaty ache. And then it came. The drama.

'Pól is fully after Megan.' Joan's voice was soft and small, as if she wasn't speaking to Muireann at all. There was a sing-song quality to the cadence as though she were reminding herself, or praying, maybe. It was hard to know how to respond. Muireann didn't want to talk about this now. Or any other time. But she had to say something.

She settled for a non-committal 'Mmm.'

Joan turned to Muireann. 'You know they all went off to Emma's gaff without us?' She didn't sound annoyed. Just stating facts.

'Yeah, I know.' Muireann shrugged, keeping her face as neutral as she could.

'I just . . . I just wish my friends were my friends, you know? It's so fucking complicated. And it isn't that complicated to be sound.'

'Mmm,' again. It was a diplomatic sort of noise. Almost soothing.

'You know I got with Pól when we went up to the house on Inishbofin?'

Muireann turned to Joan sharply. 'I didn't know that.' This was the kind of thing that would have been discussed if it were common knowledge.

Joan looked sad. 'Well we did. I didn't say because he didn't, like, change the way he was around me or anything after. I mean, I didn't think he'd be my, like, boyfriend or anything but . . . oh sure lookit . . . I don't know . . .'

The canal was black and thick-looking, like tar. The moon was waxing. The path was all lit up by golden streetlights, and Muireann thought of that weekend, in Shannon's mother's house, where they lay in the garden and howled up at the moon and drank vodka. When everybody else had gone to bed, herself and Natalie had gone down to the beach and taken off their clothes and run into the waves, and it had been so dark, true island dark, that Muireann had thought, *We could die here*, but it hadn't been a bad thing, only a primal one, and before they'd gotten dressed, they had hugged each other fiercely and it had felt like every part of her had woken up.

'When did it happen?' Muireann said.

'I don't really remember.' Joan's voice was low. 'I went up to bed, and I could hear everyone chatting, and Oisín and Shannon had their guitars out, and Natalie was singing. And I knew that Pól was after Megan, because if you look at somebody long enough, you notice things, and I fell asleep and when I woke up, he was in my bed, asking me if I was awake.'

Muireann looked at Joan.

'Joan,' she said, 'Joan. What happened?' She tried to keep her voice as even as she could.

Joan's eyes widened and she flapped her hands, as if trying to dispel the sense that something happened that was not okay. 'Oh, it wasn't like that.' She swallowed. 'I did . . . I wanted him to kiss me. I wanted him to touch me. But I knew that he was only in there with me because he knew I liked him. And it felt like a present the island was giving me, but also a secret. Like, he didn't spend the night in my room. He said he was going out for a smoke and I lay there expecting him, expecting him.' She shrugged, and tried to smile. It didn't work.

'And then yourself and Natalie came back from' – she gestured vaguely – 'wherever you were, and I heard his voice and yours, and I knew he wasn't coming back. Not for me. And it isn't some big tragedy or anything, you know? Like, I have a brain. And I could see it coming. But I felt it. Here.' Joan held a hand to the bottom of her stomach.

Muireann put her hands in her pockets and felt the stickiness of Joan's saliva on the soft wool of her hat. When Natalie had given it to her, it had been beautiful.

Joan was still speaking. 'And here. Behind my eyes. Like this feeling of really, really wanting just to cry, but not being able to. You know?'

Muireann nodded. She did know.

'And Megan is great. I know why he likes her. She's skinny and the kind of quiet where it's not shy, it's more she only speaks when she has something to say. And we look alike, but I'm the duller and more awkward version, you know?' She sighed.

There was a seagull bobbing on the water, adult sized, but speckled like an egg. Joan threw it a chip. Muireann felt that she should say something, but she had no idea what it was. Her skin felt strange, as though it belonged to someone else.

'I didn't know, Joan', she said. 'Obviously. And I'm sorry. It sounds . . . hard.'

Joan shrugged. 'Not really. But . . . I just wanted someone to know it happened. Because if I hadn't been there, I'd think I was imagining it. Or that it was a dream. But there was a condom in the bin and I took it out and wrapped it up in toilet paper and put it in the paper bag that my prescription came in from Boots.'

Muireann nodded. She licked a finger and it still tasted of Natalie, sugar, aniseed.

'It's complicated having friends,' she told Joan, 'but I do think he could have been nicer to you.'

Joan shook her head. 'No. No. I mean, I get what you mean. But . . . even though he has the capacity to be nice, I don't think he could have been nicer to me. There's something in me that he doesn't like. I think it's that I want him. You know, that hunger? That feeling like he could have me. It makes him . . . not exactly dislike me, but . . .'

Muireann made sure that her voice was measured. 'You mean he's ambivalent?'

Joan smiled. 'Thank you. Ambivalent! That's it. He is deeply ambivalent about me. And I am very not ambivalent about him. And I thought that if I met someone else, someone good, you know, that it would show him that I didn't care and maybe I, like, wouldn't care as much, or I'd be distracted.'

'Aidan?' Muireann murmured.

'Yeah. Aidan. But it's like . . . I don't even fancy him all that much. I mean, I do a bit, but as a tool to show Pól I don't care, he just felt so important, and I knew it was weird to keep going back and keep drinking so much. I even made myself sick halfway through the night so I'd be able to keep drinking and not black out.'

'Is that even a thing?' It made a sort of sense, she supposed.

'Oh, yeah, it works. It's not a perfect system, but in a pinch . . .' Joan shrugged, and Muireann felt a combination of warmth and distaste. She ate another chip and trailed her hand against a thin black railing. She could feel the paint flaking off, and she was suddenly conscious of the weight of the foundation on her skin, the pinch of underwire against her ribcage. Her fanciest bra was on its last legs. She looked over her shoulder at the path behind them and saw the vague shape of a man following along.

'Is he . . . ?' Her voice was low.

Joan nodded. 'Since the chipper. I don't think he's going to do anything. He would have started hassling us already.'

Muireann turned back. 'I am so sick of this, you know? Of this. This fucking bra. And Pól, and what he did, and now, like, can we live?'

Joan swallowed. 'That's the thing, isn't it, though, like? Sometimes we can't. And we just have to bite down and get through it.' Her eyes were filling up. 'Ugh,' she said. 'I never fucking cry. I don't know why I'm at it now. Sometimes it feels like everything is poison. Including me. And I try to fight that in myself, you know, but then you carry all this stupid hope around. And hope is what will get you. Every time.'

'It's okay,' Muireann told her, but her eyes were on the guy, who was getting closer, gaining on them. 'Are you going to talk to Pól about it?'

Joan blinked. 'No. I just think . . . it was nice. Like, the sex. It wasn't amazing, but it was nice, you know? And there was this moment when our stomachs touched and we both laughed and it felt like the most connected I've ever been with him, you know? Maybe with anyone. It felt like we were kind of . . . better friends now. And then, the way he was after. I just feel that the more I push it, the more it would take away from the niceness of it, and I just want him to leave me with something.'

Muireann swallowed. 'I do get it,' she said. 'And you get to decide. You know, like, not what happens with him and you. But, like, what you do.'

Joan shrugged. 'He gets to act, and I get to respond. And I hate it. This waiting and this wanting. It makes me feel I'm just this gaping hole, you know? This need. And I'm not. Like, not every day. But the thing with him is humming under the surface, and it's making me more and more uncomfortable with everyone as well. Like, they all prefer him to me.'

Joan was saying an awful lot of things, and that guy, with the shirt and the Converse. There was something a little off about him. She'd felt it in the chipper and she felt it more strongly now. A sort of want. She looked down at her feet. It would be hard to run but she could manage it. Joan did marathons, her whole family did, because of her mother and the cancer. Muireann was more of a light-a-candle girl, but it was amazing how quickly you could move if you needed to. Of course, there were times you couldn't move at all. Bodies were strange like that. The boy had stopped and was looking over the railing at the seagull, who was still bobbing there, a big soft comma.

'Hey!' Joan shouted.

And his whole body startled.

'Hey, are you following us?'

He shook his head.

Muireann rolled her eyes. She just wanted to get home. She wanted Joan to stop talking about what happened. She knew, she knew it was her job to listen, but the knowing made things so much more complicated and she could already see how it would go. Joan would ask her not to tell anyone, and she wouldn't want to tell anyone, but someone, probably Natalie, would sense that she knew something they didn't, and they'd start in on her until she told them. And it would hurt Megan, and Joan was right, everyone did kind of prefer Pól. They all loved Oisín anyway – he was a dote – and Pól had been his best friend since they were in junior infants and so Joan would be nudged gently out. There wouldn't be an official decision about it, but that's what would happen, now that she had told, and they both knew it.

Muireann hated how easily people could tell when she was keeping secrets, but only when it suited them of course.

'AND WHY NOT?' Joan yelled. 'WE'RE LOVELY AND WE'VE CHIPS.'

Oh Jesus Christ! Muireann squared her shoulders. She hated being the less drunk one. The sensible one. But she also kind of hated Joan. I mean, they'd had this moment of connection, or revelation or whatever, and then she decided to be a dose again, belligerent and full of chips and vodka.

The boy mumbled something. He was coming closer and now Muireann could see that his cheeks weren't flushed any more. The glow of the street light cast shadows in the hollows of his cheeks.

'What did you say?' Joan asked him, at a reasonable volume.

The boy held up a chip between a finger and a thumb. 'I also have chips. But they've gone cold now.' His voice wasn't that low, and there was something lilting, childlike, in it. He scuffed his shoe against the path and Muireann felt the threat ease in her stomach.

'Do you want to walk with us?' Joan asked. 'We're going back to Muireann's, but it's ages away yet.'

Muireann looked at her and muttered, 'Thanks, Joan.'

The boy shrugged.

Above them stars were glowing, cold and fierce and distant. Joan looked at Muireann in an intense way, widening her eyes, and Muireann sighed. She didn't know what the weird subtext to this was, whether Joan was trying to, like, get with this person to prove a point to Pól, who wouldn't care, or whether she was just sick of only having Muireann, who was boring, there to talk to. Whatever it was, she wasn't feeling it. She rubbed her hands over her cheeks and shuddered.

'I can go . . .' the boy said. 'I mean . . .' He looked down at his feet.

The waters rippled, deep and dark and lonely, and for a second Muireann saw it too, what Joan had seen.

'No,' she said. 'No, stay. Walk with us.' She smiled and elbowed Joan. 'Do you know Pól?'

Joan kicked her.

'No,' he said. 'Is he like one of these guys' – he gestured to a street light – 'or a person?'

'He wishes he was a streetlight,' Muireann said. 'He's not a good person. He slept with Joan and now he's ignoring her.'

'Muireann!' Joan's mouth was open.

'What? You didn't tell me not to tell anyone.' Muireann uncrossed her arms, stretched them wide.

'*Yet*. I didn't tell you not to tell anyone *yet*. I was obviously going to.'

The boy smiled, but it didn't reach his eyes. 'I'm not sure that I count. I mean, I don't really know who you're talking about, and I'm not one hundred percent sure that I'm a person.'

'What are you talking about?' Joan said. 'Of course you're a person.'

Muireann nodded. 'Everybody is. Except for Pól.'

The boy looked dubious but made a sound that could have been agreement. They walked along together. Muireann crumpled up her bag but couldn't see a bin. The boy reached out his hand for it, folded it and placed it in his own bag. Joan held out her bag for him to do the same, which was pure Joan behaviour, but she smiled warmly at him as she did it, and Muireann could see something relaxing in his bearing.

It wasn't, she realised, in any way sexual. Joan hadn't adjusted the way she held herself, wasn't making more eye contact than she needed to, which was a relief, as Muireann really didn't want to bring two people home who were going to end up riding on the sofa. Orlagh and Fiachra would probably call a house meeting. They were a year older than her and there was a bang of parent off them sometimes that she really didn't appreciate.

'What are you thinking about, Muireann?'

'Just Orlagh and Fiachra.' Muireann shivered. Jesus, it was cold.

'Do you think they'll mind us coming back with you?' Joan asked.

Muireann was weirdly fine with the unspoken decision that he was theirs to mind till the morning.

'Oh, no. I can go . . . I don't want to be . . . ' he said, and his face looked very young all of a sudden.

'It's fine,' Muireann said. 'The more the merrier. As long as more is three people or less. Otherwise my housemates will get grumpy. There'll be notes.'

'Sure, I thought they were always partying,' Joan said.

Muireann sighed. 'They are. But they've the same friends, so when they do it it's fine.'

'Sometimes I'm really glad I live at home.' Joan turned to the boy. 'What's your name?'

There was a pause, and then he told them. 'Ciarán.' He rubbed his chin. His hands were very small. Muireann wanted to ask where he lived, but something told her just to leave it so. His eyes were bloodshot. There was no one with him. Even back at Shakes there hadn't been. Muireann shivered, but not from the cold. Last year, they'd pulled three young lads out of the canal. Two of them might have been the drink, but the third was definitely going through some stuff. Muireann had read about it. There had been a vigil. She hadn't gone but she'd seen them huddling with their candles on her way to work. She'd blessed herself. She wasn't that religious at all really, but sometimes you just needed to do something. They turned up by the bakery, past the little crèche with the red gate.

'Not too far to go now,' Joan told him. 'I'm looking forward to a cup of tea.'

'Me too,' said Muireann.

Ciarán shrugged. 'I don't really drink tea. I know it's weird, but hot drinks just feel wrong to me.'

Muireann smiled. 'That's fair. There are lots of different ways to be.' She took her phone out, scrolled through her messages. There were a few from Natalie, telling her to try and ditch Joan and come to Emma's. She left it on read because she wasn't sure what to say back. She didn't want to get into bitching about Joan while she was walking right beside her. Tomorrow it would all start seeping in again. She turned the screen off, slid the phone into her bag.

'Is everything okay?'

'Yeah. Yeah, it is.' She smiled at Joan, at Ciarán. They turned to walk through the estate. She wouldn't take that shortcut on her own, but there were three of them.

'Are you sure it's okay?' Ciarán asked again. 'Like . . . ye don't know me.'

His face looked pained. When Muireann was small, they'd gotten a rescue dog. His name was Leon, and he hid under a table in the shed for days. He wasn't used to light. To being loved. There were marks on his neck from being chained. And bit by bit, they slowly won him round, but there was always something there that still remembered, quick to quiver, snap, expect the worst. They'd put him down eventually. They kind of had to.

Joan shrugged.

'That's probably a good thing. Sure we're more likely to get sexually assaulted by people we know. Statistically.'

Muireann startled, murmured, 'Jesus, Joan.'

Ciarán looked at her, and held her gaze. 'I mean, I think you're fairly safe with me, girls. But, like, I don't think people who do that sort of thing generally advertise it, like.'

Muireann made a non-committal noise. 'No, they wouldn't do. I mean, it would defeat the purpose.' She tried to smile but kind of stopped halfway.

'Everybody thinks that they're a good person,' Joan said, and her eyebrows furrowed. 'But I don't know that many people who are. I know I'm not.'

'Ah, Joan,' Muireann said. 'You're not that bad, in fairness.'

'I shouldn't have stirred things up, about the earrings. It was none of my business. It's just . . . she's always getting away with shit, you know?'

'Everyone is,' Ciarán said. 'But for what it's worth, you both seem nice. A bit weird but nice.' He smiled, and Muireann felt herself exhale.

'Thanks for the assessment, Ciarán.' Joan rolled her eyes.

'Yeah,' said Muireann. 'Typical fucking Ciarán.'

They were approaching the house now. Muireann scrambled for her keys and wondered if they were foolish to not be afraid of letting him in. He was, after all, a stranger, and they couldn't know whether or not he was the kind of person who would steal things, break things, hurt things. Later, she would wonder if Ciarán could read that on her face, because as they reached the door, he moved away.

'I think I'll head,' he said. 'It was nice to meet ye. Really. Thank you.' But he lingered.

'Sure, we did nothing,' Joan said, smiling with a warmth that reminded Muireann of her mother.

Ciarán turned away, and there was something so vulnerable in the slant of his back that Muireann wished she could take all her doubt back. Just be sound. She reached a hand out to him.

'Do you, like, do you want to come in and wait for a taxi or something?' She tried to smile. It didn't really take.

'Nah,' he said. 'Sure, I know the way I'm going. Slán, girls.'

Ciarán raised a hand. They looked at him. He looked back. Neither of the girls moved. He swallowed. 'I'll be okay,' he said. 'It's just a weird time. And I appreciate ye being kind.'

'Sure we did nothing,' Joan said again, and Muireann shrugged and smiled. He didn't speak again. Just walked away. Underneath the street lights he seemed to stretch taller, shining golden. He slowly turned the corner, disappeared.

'I shouldn't have said that' – Joan closed the door – 'about the sexual assault. I was trying to be funny or something.'

'No,' Muireann said. 'It was pretty accurate, in fairness.'

'I don't know,' Joan said. 'I'll put the kettle on.' She ran her fingers through her hair. 'None of them messaged me to see if I was okay. And I wasn't, like. I mean I'm not. I spat into your beanie. Out of spite, like.'

'Yeah, I noticed.' Muireann crooked her mouth.

'I mean, I just . . . I'd like people to care. And maybe I need to care more for that to happen.' She went over to the fridge to get the milk.

'Do you think he'll be okay, Muireann?' Joan's face was strangely twisted. And Muireann knew, maybe for the first time, exactly how she felt. There was a sense that they had very nearly made a difference, that there was so much more they could have done, if only they were other sorts of people.

'I don't know.' Her voice was small, almost a whisper.

Joan looked at her for a long time before she spoke again. And when she did, it was like she couldn't stop herself. A rush. A river.

'The thing is that once someone's gone, they're gone. They don't come back. My mam . . . she used to tell me about when I was born, and it was just me and her in hospital together. And I would only sleep on her chest. And she said when a baby comes into the world first, it doesn't know yet how to be a person. It reaches for the comfort of the womb. The smell of home. She got . . . she got a bit like that on the way out . . . before it went entirely downhill. She'd always be trying to tell me these stories and to give me these memories she held, and I didn't listen well enough, you know? I would be looking at her hair growing back, or her bones all jutting through her skin, and just feeling the taste of death inside my mouth. The tang of it. The fear. Because she was my home . . . and now . . .' She shook her head. 'I'm drunk. And I'm ridiculous. But there was something lonely about Ciarán. And I knew how he felt. And I just wish . . . I don't know what I wish.'

Muireann nodded slowly. Outside the window she saw the cloths that Fiachra had left outside on the bush for some strange reason. They wouldn't dry much there, and it was still quite dark, but soon the light would start to filter through, finger by finger, and they would see the washing line, the little lilac tree. This place had been somebody else's house at some point, and they were probably dead now, or in a nursing home. And when Muireann left, some other person would move in, take her place. And her mother didn't really tell her stories, not like that, probably because she felt that they had time. But when Muireann had been home for the Christmas, she'd given her a medal when she was leaving.

'This is for you,' she'd said, 'to keep you safe.'

It was just a little bit of metal. But she kept it with her all the same.

She took a slug of tea and met Joan's eyes. 'I can't even imagine. That sounds so hard, but also like you loved her and she loved you.'

'I did love her.' Joan said. 'I loved her very much. She was my mam, you know? And if there was a way, like, anything at all, I would have done it.'

They sat opposite each other, drinking tea from the thick ceramic mugs Orlagh had made in her pottery module, which needed to be handwashed carefully, and Muireann felt an urge to tell Joan about the time that Pól had come into her room, after Emma's birthday party last year. And how he didn't act differently around her after either, but how she kept a chair against her door now. And if it wasn't there, she couldn't sleep. It hadn't been a big dramatic thing. Like, you wouldn't call the guards. She hadn't anyway. And he probably had no idea, none, how she felt now. Some people just . . . it was like the world was for them, for the taking. And every now and then, he'd smile at her like they'd a secret, and she hated that. But there was nothing she could do. Not now, not yet. And if she told Joan, she knew that Joan would hear her and believe her, but also it would make it very real. It was simpler just to keep on going as she had been. She didn't think about it every day. Not any more.

'You know what Ciarán said before,' Muireann asked, 'about not really being a person?'

'Yeah,' said Joan.

'I kind of knew what he meant.' And this time her voice cracked. She let it crack.

'Yeah,' said Joan again. 'Yeah. Me too, Muireann.'

She reached across the pine to hold her hand.

I grew up near the sea, and whenever I'm away from water, I miss it. When I'm in the sea, it feels like home, but not necessarily a home where I feel welcome or safe. The sea is a wild, brutal thing, and though its beauty can take your breath away, so too can its power. Spring equinox had me thinking about balance – day and night, earth and water, fear and love. Selkie stories have that aspect too – the liminal creature, balancing gracefully between two worlds, is forced into exile and tethered to the land by the love of her children. The lure of the sea is generally too powerful, and in the end, she may kill them by taking them with her, or hurt them by abandoning them. I wanted to write about the period before a choice is made, and to look at that dance between desperation, trauma and the depth of love.

The sun is shining and the air is cold. I am playing with my wooden farm. The cow and the sheep and the pig and the horse and the duck are lined up in the field. I move the tractor around the barn, once, twice, three times. I am looking at the farm, but I am listening to Mammy. The sounds she makes, the ones she doesn't know I understand. I cannot make them, even when I try my very hardest. Our throats are different.

I got this farm for Christmas. It came wrapped in a big box, and Dad wanted me to open it first so he could see me love it. He likes it when we smile. Mammy tries to smile when Dad's here. She isn't smiling now, though. I try my very best to keep it quiet. She is getting ready to do baking. She has everything all lined up. White flour, brown flour, baking soda, buttermilk and oil. Oil doesn't mix with water. She showed me in a glass. It floats on top.

I put all of the animals in a shoebox that I painted red. It was black before, so we had to cover it with paper. Mammy's hands were happier that day.

I watch her work, slapping at the dough over and over. Twisting it like it's done something bad. Her back is to me and her shoulders are up almost to her ears. She sounds like a dog who wants something. She sounds like the front door Dad has to fix. She cuts a cross into the tops and puts them in the oven. Then she rubs my back and plays with me. She is quieter but her face is sad.

When the loaves are ready, she puts one of them on the windowsill to cool. Once Shep stole a loaf, but Dad beat him for it, so he probably won't do that again. We will have it later with the dinner, when Dad gets home. He has been gone a while, out on the boats, but he is coming back. He always does. He tells me to be careful around Shep. You never know with dogs, when they will bite. But I love Shep. He has a warm back and a lot of hair. Mammy lets me rub him all the time and that's a secret, like the second loaf.

The second loaf is warm and the inside of it is all wet and crumbly. Mammy pulls at it with her hands. I reach for some, she bats my hand away. It's all for her. One by one, she eats the chunks of bread, washed right down with milk. The butter drips down on the tablecloth. I sit and watch. I do not annoy her. When she's done, she wipes the table with her hand and eats the crumbs and drips, and licks her palm until there's nothing left. She reaches out a hand to stroke my hair, and then she tells me what she always tells me.

'It isn't that I'm hungry. I'm just cold.'

I know she is. I feel it too. The same. Mam picks around her fingernails and pulls off a big white strip of skin. I see the red of blood. I get a bandage from the little press and give it to her. She takes it from me, nods and calls me good. I try hard to be good. I want her to stay with us. With me. I reach my arms out wide like Little Nutbrown Hare and I wrap them around her legs. They aren't cold at all, but on the outside everything is grand. It's on the inside Mammy feels it hurting. I look up at her and she looks down at me. She's wearing three cardigans today. Her eyes are shiny dark. The sea at night. And she is strong and soft and beautiful and mine. She smells like home, like warm skin and milk.

I like it now. When it's just the two of us together. Rónán goes to school because he is big. He's her boy and I'm her little pup – that's what she calls me. People think it means I give her cheek. And sometimes I do, but that is not exactly what it is. We are the same sort of thing, Mammy and me. When I place my head against her chest, our hearts are quick together, *thump thump.*

She breathes me in, and I feel her fingers tangle in my hair. People always say things about my hair, because it's white. It won't be white for ever. Rónán's was like that but it went brown, Dad says. I don't want to change. To be too big. I want to stay small so she has to mind me. Keep me safe. I reach my hands up to tug on her long braid and her dark eyes meet mine. She scoops a spoon of butter into her mouth and I butt my head against her breast. We laugh and I am not cold any more.

I only get milk once a day now, and not when Dad is home. He thinks I am too big to drink from Mammy. 'Animal,' he says and shakes his head, but I don't care. At night I'm not allowed and when I wake I can't go back to sleep without my mammy. I suck my wrist and listen to the sea against the rocks. Last night the moon was round and shiny like a flashlight and I got up and looked out of the window. It was still too dark to see the rocks. There are six of them, all different shapes. 'They could lift their heads up and be dinosaurs one day,' Rónán says, but I'm not scared of anything at all but losing Mammy. When I'm big I can swim out to them all by myself.

Dad doesn't want me learning to swim. His eyebrows go right down into his eyes when he says that if I learn to swim, someday I'll drown. Mammy says that isn't how it works, she'll teach me anyway. Another secret for us both to keep. She wipes the counters down and gives me a little pot of yoghurt and some apple. We get my jacket and my woolly hat.

When Dad was a boy, he was on the boats with Grandad, and now he's on the boats with Uncle Aindréas. He always knew he wanted to be a fisherman. 'It's a hard life,' he says, 'but it's the only life I want.' When he tucks me in, he talks to me like that. I rub his scratchy chin and hairy arms and feel salt on my skin, a big net, fat with bodies. Dad is scary sometimes but he loves us.

When he's gone, it's Rónán, me and Mammy. The house is ours, but then when he comes back it's his again. He always says he's happy to be home and that he missed us. And then he looks around for things that changed. A vase, a cup, a smile. Dad likes the house to stay the way he left it, but it is like the sea, things always move. When I touch Mammy's skin, sometimes I feel a flicker, or a gasp. A different sort of sting. A hurt that lingers. I look at her and want to cry but it's not my sad, it's hers, it just spills out, it's too much for one person. Like when you don't turn off the tap in time. We head out. I'm in my blue boots with the diggers on them. They were Rónán's once upon a time.

Maisie and baby Niamh go by us with the buggy. They're going to the playground or the shops. I do a little wave and Maisie smiles and asks my mother how she is. She makes a little hum and tilts her head. She doesn't sound like other people do, so she doesn't talk that much outside the house. The sound of her makes people's faces change. They get all itchy. When Dad is there they talk to him instead.

The days are getting longer now. When I eat my dinner, the sun is there. Soon it will be there when I go to bed as well. I follow Mammy, filling my bucket up with seaweed, shells. Mammy looks at what I've got, picks out the ones that aren't good to eat. She nuzzles the side of my face with her soft nose, and I snuggle her back. I hear the water moving on the rocks. I hear the wind. And she is here beside me and I'm safe. If my two arms were strong, I would grab Mammy, keep her here with me, the way that Dad did. She wants to go. I don't want her to go.

We are the only people on the beach. Sometimes people walk their dogs here, and then we have to wait for them to leave. Mammy nods at me, takes off her clothes. She folds them very carefully and we put them in a little bag that we cover up with sand and sticks of driftwood so nobody will steal them. We leave our towels folded on a rock. She holds me in her arms as she swims out. I can't swim as far or fast as Mammy. She doesn't want to wait for me but she doesn't want to leave me either. So she plops me on the flattest rock, and then she goes away into the water. I stay where I am. I have no choice. If I cry out, she will not hear me. I lie flat and look up at the clouds. The wind is hard and cold, the waves are high. I like walking to the shore with Mammy, having secrets with her. I like seeing her swim. How strong she is.

In the house, being by myself is not so bad. There are toys and books. I can move around. But on the rock, inside the sea, is different. Mammy belongs to it and not to me. I bite my lip and wait for her to come. And I think about the day she won't. It's not today — I see her head flick up, her roundy nose, dark eyes. She's gasping air in, flopping like a fish. She grasps the edge of the rock and I can see the anger in her eyes. Mammy gets angry in a different way to Dad. He throws his anger out, all over people. Mammy just fills up with hers, and I don't see it going anywhere the way Dad's does. She doesn't slap or shout or kick a chair. Sometimes she'll put things down on counters really loudly, clatter pots, and make these sounds that aren't even words, under her breath. When the sky is grey and the air is pressing down, sometimes I can feel a storm coming in my shoulders and my tummy, heavy, heavy. And it's a bit like that with Mammy, and with Dad. Only the storm never comes with Mammy. I watch her, wary, as she hauls on up.

'It's not enough, puppy,' she tells me. And I can see the water in her eyes, the reflection of it and also lines of it all down her cheeks. She swallows. And I know that this will be the part I hate. My turn to try. She curls her legs beneath her and rubs a hand across her hair to get some little strands out of her face. I look up at Mammy and down at the waves. I know what she wants me to do and I want to make her happy so I push myself off the rock, slide in, and just let go.

Mammy says that she used to be different. Her body changed with every year on land. The net keeps tightening around her and inside her. She says she used to have a way of sucking loads of air into her lungs, and holding it all in, a trick with nostrils, tongue. When we are here, she talks about stuff more, she tells me things. There was a time she wasn't let be near the sea at all, in case she'd run. After she had Rónán, she was allowed go back, but her body had forgotten how to hold breath for a long, long time. She hopes that if she stays down long enough, then something will kick in. It will remember. She wants my body to remember too; she thinks it might because I come from her, but I don't know. I stay down for as long as I can, and I look at seaweed in the salty water. I don't see anyone under the waves. I don't think she did either. I can hear the blood inside my body while I wait until it's long enough. Dilisk. Carrageen. Horned wrack. Mermaid's hair. The Little Mermaid wanted to go on land and meet a prince. My mammy didn't but she had to anyway. My chest is sore, but I still stay down. I try my best.

When Mammy was little, she had fluffy hair as well, all over her body. It was white. She had her family around her then, but now they are all gone. Because of what happened to her. If she wanted to go off and find them, she'd have to be able to swim the way she did before everything, and she would want to take me with her too because I am her puppy and she loves me, and that's a sort of trap that Dad has made. I need to try my very best for Mammy. I don't want her to leave me on my own.

Every time I try to put my head back up, her strong hand pushes back. I cannot breathe. I can see dots, and saltwater is in my lungs, my eyes. It's filling me. I start to fight her, bite and thrash. Then up she pulls me with her two strong arms. I sob and scream at her. She strokes my hair and both of us are crying. 'I don't like doing this to you,' she says. 'But I can't leave you with him.' She looks at me. 'I would kill you first. But I could never do that either, puppy. So we keep on trying, so we do.'

I nod, but I remember the feeling of her hand pushing my head. I know what she wants, how much she wants it. I don't think she would kill me, but the sea might. It doesn't know she loves me. It doesn't sing to Mammy any more. She used to be able to swim so far away, but now she's stuck here and, one way or another, she needs to get out of it and back to somewhere else. It is killing her. She cannot breathe. Her skin is dry and cracking, open wounds. She talks like that when she's washing dishes, mopping the floor, changing bedsheets. Not in the words that other people use, but in her words, that sort of way that's a bit like singing and a bit like screaming and a bit like whistling.

She helps me back to shore, and we dress, brush the sand from our skin and out of our hair. She will run a hot bath when we're home, like she always does, and we will sit together, the warmth coming back into our blood. Mammy's mouth is bluey-grey. Her hands are shaking. I look up at her and I love her. And I would want to keep her in my house. Even if she didn't want to be there.

Dad tells the story of how they met sometimes when he's been drinking. How she was on a rock in the sunshine with her sisters, and Dad fell in love with her the minute he saw her and knew that he had to take her home with him to be his wife, and have his babies. Uncle Aindréas says no one else would have him, and people laugh, but Dad's face is always serious. He says he would have done anything, anything at all to make her his. He gives Mammy a rub, and I can see the sea inside her eyes.

Mammy never tells the story out loud, but sometimes I get pictures in my head that hurt my heart. It isn't like the way that Dad said, but very different, all in feelings, flashes. Moments here and there, the way she startles when someone brushes past her unexpectedly. The way sometimes her eyes pull curtains in her head and she is gone. The sounds she makes when she wakes up from nightmares. They all draw me a picture of his face. His two eyes fixed on her. His arms. His knife.

After the bath, Mammy will give me my lunch and then she will do housework and I will help her out, and play some more, and I will think about the darkness under the waves just before I drank that breath of air and I will feel afraid, and I will go upstairs and look for Mammy and she will be staring out the window at the path that leads us right back to the sea. And I will tug her T-shirt and I will ask if tomorrow we can go to the playground instead, and she will nod her head but we will go back to the sea again. We always do.

In the stories people tell about women like Mammy, they have a magic cloak, but Mammy didn't have a cloak at all. I don't think that there is such a thing as a magic cloak like that. But it is a nicer picture to make inside your head than Mammy's pelt. Sometimes when she yelps and yips, I see it like she's telling it to me. The story. How he had to cut the seal part off of her, to peel her like an orange. And what he took from her is not hidden in the rafters or out the back under all the piles of chopped-up wood. He left it where it was, and it was pecked by birds, and then it rotted, and stank up the beach. Kept the rest away, so she had no one, no one, and he was on her and in her and we were in her and on her and she can't get away. Her home is gone, and she can see him making Rónán like him. See herself pushing her boy away, making a pet of me, but she can't stop it, even when she tries to, nothing works. And she just wants to go back to before, to go back home, but the part of her that had a home is dead now. And all there is, is this. But it's too much, and she can't leave me here alone with them, though something in her sings that day will dawn. So she bakes bread, and eats it up in secret, and fish and mussels, little ocean-things. And every day, she takes me by the hand so we can practise being underwater, in case one day our bodies shift and change as they remember all that was forgotten, fat and strong and graceful as the sea wraps her two arms around us and says, 'It's okay, it's okay, Mammy's here, don't cry, don't cry, you're safe now, you're with me, come here, come drink my milk. I love you, and I'm going nowhere, puppy, I'm your home. You're home. You're home with me.'

Protection rituals, ways of carving space, of feeling safe in your skin or in your home, have always appealed to me, and May is a good time for boundary keeping. Many of the traditional practices around Bealtaine were around warding off threats, mundane and otherworldly. New motherhood is a time that mirrors that for me, where in the wake of labour, you are tasked with keeping safe something that doesn't seem to be quite of the world yet. Time moves differently. There's a sense of elation tempered with vigilance, with worry. We all want to be capable of protecting ourselves and those we love, and the realisation that, to a great extent we aren't is hard to bear. So we put yellow flowers across thresholds, and we love each other and we hope.

—

In this house we are, above all things, careful. When food falls on the floor, we do not pick it up. It's their food now. We sprinkle holy water round the rooms, and keep a mountain ash branch on the lowest shelf inside the door of the fridge, beside the milks. Skimmed enriched with vitamins for you, full-fat for her, and hazelnut for me. We have a special locked box for the breast milk. It isn't very big. I don't pump much. We just want to be safe. To keep them safe.

It's just past noon. I wipe the counters down and Milton everything, then boil the kettle, make a cup of tea. He wakes up from his nap just as I'm poised to drink it. I don't mind that. I love him in my arms. She's still in crèche. I leave the tea to cool, settle in the cosy armchair, and put him to my breast. His mouth moves and I feel the latch, the pull. Breastfeeding has been easier this time around. When she was born, the pain was something else. I was in bits. The PHN said to count for twenty seconds and if it felt like needles after that, then there was something wrong. I would bite my lip and watch the TV, counting, counting. Eyes closed, jaw clenched, the warm little huddle of her in my arms, working at my flesh, wearing me raw.

Fiche

There'd been two other houses that we'd gone sale agreed on. Both fell through. We despaired, and she was in my belly and we didn't have a garden, or a room the right size for a baby. I felt like we were failing her, would stroke my stomach and scroll through houses we didn't have a hope of getting when I couldn't sleep. I'd send you link after link. Two beds, three beds, anything at all. Back then, we weren't sure that we would even want another baby. We wanted first to meet the one we had. Now sometimes I search for the houses we missed out on, go on satellite view, look in windows, gardens. I don't know what I want to find there. A version of our life that isn't this.

A naoi déag

This place was isolated, needed work, but some of the rooms were perfectly liveable. It had been built from a catalogue in the seventies, on the site of a much older house. There was an acre of land around it, thick stone boundary walls. Connection to the mains, water supply, the roof was in good shape, and the foundations. All the boxes ticked, but I was looking at the little wrought-iron gate, the hawthorn tree, the orchard, the lilacs, and the little robin flitting round the walls. I turned to you and said, 'She owns the place.' You smiled at me. 'For now.' You touched my stomach, and the baby kicked. Everything was soft and quick like that, an antidote to slowness, disappointment. I kept waiting for the panic to hit me, for everything to crumble in my hands. It didn't. We got movers, made it work. I found a new GP, changed hospitals. I took my maternity leave as early as I could. Made phone calls, sorted plumbers, electricians. Made colour-coded lists as we got used to the house, its quirks and flaws. I rubbed my stomach and I made her promises. I wanted her to have so many things. The whole wide world.

A hocht déag

I change his nappy, then put him in his rocker while I hoover. He looks at me with milky baby eyes. And I remember when her eyes were that way too. Little pools, or pockets of the sky. I think a baby's mostly overwhelmed. This world can be a lot, for any person. I want to tell him that he is the best little boy in the whole world. That Mammy loves his kicky little legs. But we don't do that now. We've learned to hold our tongues. I finish up. Put him in the baby gym, hang up the small giraffe, the little bell. He reaches for them. I play peek-a-boo with him. He doesn't get it, but he likes my face, my voice, my closeness. His fingers grab the giraffe by the legs. He smiles. It's new. His little smile is new. I swallow down the praise. I stroke his tummy.

A seacht déag

Pregnancy with her was kind to me. My hair the fullest it has ever been, my skin was clear. From the outside I was blooming, blooming. Everybody told me things like that, over video chat, and later when we could have outdoor meet-ups. I smiled and nodded, but I felt afraid. I had this sense that something bad would happen. On the radio they said wear masks. Wash hands. Stay apart. Be careful. I worked from home, which eased my mind a bit. My sister kept telling me to get out, go out, do things. 'You won't be able to once she is born.' I kept reminding her that it wasn't that simple, what with lockdown. I went for little walks in the morning and the evening, to bookend work hours, made slightly nicer dinners I couldn't really stomach in the end. We planned, we problem-solved, we bought a house. That was an achievement, I suppose. It seemed like one. And we pretend we're happy here, of course. Whenever we're in company. The truth would be a dangerous thing to tell.

A sé déag

I put him in the Boba Wrap and I get the bucket. Gather up the yellow flowers. The gorse, the cowslip, primrose. Not too much from any place or plant. The gorse is what I like the most. It's almost always blooming. It survives. And it has thorns. Can hurt. I fill my bucket and I take him home. I line the windowsills with yellow petals. Then he wakes and I feed him again. I change his nappy. He has done wees, there is a little rash, a few red spots. I lather them with Sudocrem. I have to get more Vaseline, I think. I make a note. He doesn't cry. The patience of him. She was never like that.

'You're a great little man.' I tell him. Then I catch myself. 'Pity you're so ugly.'

I smear a little bin juice on the soft top of his head. They don't like dirty things. I want to cry.

A cúig déag

When she was born, we used to tell her daily how we loved her. Because we did. My God, it hit me hard. I held her on my chest and I was crying and the midwife telling me I'd done a great job and the doctor sewing me back up, and you there looking shellshocked and this little sticky scrawny someone snuggling in, just trying to get back to where she'd been. The lights were too harsh on her, I tried to make a shadow with my hand. Her lips around my nipple, seeking, sucking. She didn't get much yet, but we were trying. And I'd been worried, because there had been so many times in my life when I couldn't feel the right thing at the right time. Childhood Christmases. Our wedding day. And this was the biggest thing we'd ever done. A person who we'd have to mind forever. 'It will be okay,' I said to her. 'It will be okay. I love you, oh, I love you.' Later, while she slept in the strange fish-tank cots they have in hospital, I said to you, 'If anybody ever, ever hurts her, I will kill them.' And you nodded. We would murder now. Something had changed. And I was glad, because for the last few weeks before, I kept on thinking of my friend Joanne who'd said she hadn't gotten that rush, that fierce connection. She'd looked at her child's face and she had thought, *Who are you how am I going to manage help me help me.*

A ceathair déag

I pick her up from crèche and place her in the second car seat. I've sewn old iron nails in little pockets all the way up his. I have iron filings in the lining of our clothes. And sometimes salt as well. Can't be too careful.

A trí déag

When she came home, the house was still a shell of sorts, but it was our shell. The bathroom was done. The kitchen-cum-living room. Our bedroom. And there was time enough for the rest of it. For there to be a shape put on the garden. I had this nice idea of raised beds. Of big hands, little ones. My mother'd grown tomatoes, spuds and peas when we were young and I had loved them. There's nothing like a pea fresh from the pod. The sweet surprise of it. It felt so easy. Our sleep was broken but we were both there. She fed a lot, but I'd expected that. She'd latch and I would count just like they said. And it was generally bearable by the time I got to twenty, and I watched every single episode of *Ru Paul's Drag Race* and drank litres and litres of what you called breas-tea.

It tasted of roots and twigs and fennel. Work still emailed me, a lot, and I sometimes replied at three a.m., and then felt guilty. This was our special time, for me and her. I kept a little notebook by the bed to track the night feeds. And that was when I felt it first. That silent hum, a bit like a vibration in the air or something very gently tuning in. I was holding her, and I looked at the little gap between the curtains. It was country dark, no chink of light. When I went to put her back in the cot, all the soft hairs on my skin were standing up. You're not supposed to co-sleep, and she was so little. So I just held her on my chest, and counted, like I had done with the latching. Waiting for the feeling to relent. The dawn came first.

A dó dhéag

I thought that we were safer here, in the beginning, away from the city. You'd need to walk a mile to even see another person's house. We got another car, in case something happened. A small grey Skoda Fabia, second-hand. I went to pick up a parcel at the depot. The man looked at the address for a long time before he handed it over. Looked at her little head inside the wrap. 'Keep her close,' he said. A pause. 'It goes so quickly.' He turned away abruptly. I stroked her head. My eyes felt hot and itchy with the tiredness. It had been a week of staying up, of straining for that hum, of keeping vigil. I needed help, but any time I tried to put it into words it just felt wrong. I called landscapers about the garden and they said they could do raised beds no bother, but they couldn't touch the hawthorn tree. I didn't want it gone, just a little place to sit beside it. To catch the sunlight when the summer came. They wouldn't budge. I held her and I looked out of the window at that tree. Gripped her so tight she started to complain.

A haon déag

I make blueberry banana muffins from the *Cook for Baba* book I got. He won't be weaned for months yet, but she loves them. I hear a shuffle outdoors and I get one of the TK Lemonade bottles of holy water from under the sink. I trace a crucifix on his forehead, hands. I drench a sponge and wipe the thresholds, windowsills and doorways, anywhere at all they could get in. He begins to grizzle and I tie a small red rag around his wrist before I take my breast out, latch him, soothe him. *We've got this down*, I think, *we will be fine*. They say you're more relaxed with your second. With the first one, everything needs to be so close to perfect. With the second you know there's no such thing. She toddles up to me and wants to grab the sponge. 'No,' I say. 'Yuk, yuk!' That's how we talk now. Nonsense words. No names. There's power in a name.

A deich

The flower buds are fat, they promise blossoms. This is the time of year when it got bad. I swallow and I look out of the window. The leaves are bright. A feral cat is sleeping in the sun. We wait until directly after sunset. I pump milk so I can get a stretch. You gather hazel rods. While the kids are still asleep, we peel the bark off, carve them into figures. Small, crude things with little sliced-out mouths. I place them in the corners of each room, and you stay up till three a.m., watching them, and searching online for a good deal on insurance. I sit and stare at the baby, feed him when he wakes, and hold him, soothe him. All is quiet. I'm straining for the hum I cannot hear.

A naoi

Before all this, I would walk down to the lake with her in her buggy and I would tell her, 'Síofra, I love you.' I would give her milk there, sitting on the grass, and sing to her and make her all these promises. But there was something listening to us both, and it followed us home. It is stealthy, subtle, but my body knows when it is there. It tells me things. I listen to it very closely these days. My skin. My spine. My ears. That hum, that hum.

A hocht

You think it might have been the hawthorn tree, but I'm sure it was the lake, and so I do not take him to the lake. Even though the sun's bright in the sky and it gleams silver. It's so hard to know what's underneath the surface of anything. Even with people. Even on land. And there are stories about something old across the waves. Hungry for the family it lost. I used to love those stories. Back then the quiet seemed peaceful. Now it's tense. A pause. We are constantly waiting for something to happen. You go into the office one day a week, but mostly you are here. We do not ever leave them on their own. Not for a second. My mother used to say that you would want eyes in the back of your head, and it's true, but not exactly in the way she meant it. 'We need to buy more salt,' I say. You nod.

A seacht

When I was little, there used to be an altar in the classroom for Mary at this time of year. Blue flowers, a statue, Rosary beads, a candle. Little treasures that we would bring in, like daisies, stones. When I look back on it, of course there was. It wasn't to honour her, not really. More to remind us that we need protection. This time of year is fat and thin at once. Clear skies, wild blooms and hungry things emerging from the wilderness. Joy is a very easy thing to steal.

A sé

With a child, you learn things as you go, black-handled knives are good to keep around. Rowan berries strung upon a thread. Some people say that sycamore's the better branch to use, but I like gorse to hang above the door. The yellow flowers, the thorns, the darkness of it. It starkly marks the boundaries of a place. When I told you what I had been doing, I felt ashamed, my tongue too big and dry inside my mouth. I couldn't look at you, but at the same time I could not keep quiet. I couldn't do this alone, not any more. It wasn't safe. You listened to me carefully, the way you always do, and when I paused, you nodded slowly, sadly. You believed me. You had felt things too. Your hands twisting at each other in your lap you told me of a night you'd woken up to the light outside blinking. You'd wanted to fix it, let me get some sleep, but when you reached the door, toolbox in hand, something told you not to pull the handle. The garden in the night-time wasn't ours. You'd be intruding where it would be foolish to intrude, and if you did there would be consequences. You thought of her there, lying in the cot, her little bum up in the air to sleep, and what flashed through your brain was, *They like children.* That's the thing we've both heard, over and over again, in stories, songs. They can't have them and they want them so they take them, and people just ignore it, until they can't. We couldn't any more. They wanted Síofra.

A cúig

It wasn't an instant thing, all of the rituals. We had to try things, listen, see what worked. That strange vibration rising, in the air and up my spine. What made it quieter? There aren't any rules, not hard and fast ones. It's trial and error. Searching for answers online. Downloading podcasts. Looking at other people's houses, what they do. When I was pregnant with the little fella, one morning I went out for a walk. We do still leave the house. I mean, you have to. I went to cross a field to take the short way home. It was just a normal field, but somehow I got lost in there for hours, trying to find a way out. I could see the house and not get to it. It was useless, until a half-remembered something from my great-aunt came back to me. I took off my clothes, turned them inside out and when I put them back on something loosened. When I reached the door, I felt for my keys and my pockets were stuffed full of hawthorn blossoms. I held my stomach in my hands and sobbed.

A ceathair

I give the boy his vitamin D drops, load the two of them into the car, begin the drive to crèche. Driving past the lake I feel my neck begin to turn around. I push it back. Keep my eyes on the road. There have been sixteen deaths on this small stretch. You cannot be too careful. If anything happened to either of us, we wouldn't be long losing him as well. That cannot happen. I fiddle with the label of my top. In the mirror, what was my daughter meets my eyes and smiles.

I don't know when her eyes began to change. Get cleverer, and cooler. Less bombarded by the glints and glimmers of the world, and more engaged. I don't know when her smile grew sharper, wider. All I know is that we did the best we could and maybe it was good enough, but there is a strong chance that it wasn't. One endless night when she was eight months old she woke up not crying but screaming. I put her to my breast to drink from me. She bit down. Drew blood. Began to suck. The next day there were all these little spots around her mouth. I was too scared to feed her, although she screamed and screamed for it. There is still a small sickle-shaped scar, around my nipple. When I see it I feel so ashamed.

A trí

We wanted answers, something definitive, a way to help her, or at least be sure. The hum had quieted now, but the fear remained. We asked around, but had to be delicate about the way we put it. You can't just say it out, a thing like this, not without consequences. We did approach a woman in the locality who has the cure for warts. We thought that she might know. We spoke in codes, but she knew what we meant. Her face grim, her make-up impeccable, blouse buttoned to the neck. She asked us why we'd ever bought that house. We said that it was cheap. She said, 'It would be.' Waved away our money. Told us to come back if we got warts.

A dó

And we could get her back, we could, we could. There are so many stories, but I can't burn her with a sod of turf, threaten her or leave her out at night. I won't be cruel to something that's the same shape as my daughter. In case all of this is just in our heads. I mean, there isn't any way to tell. Beyond that thing they say: a mother knows. Her little hands. And something in her eyes. I watch the baby and I tell myself. It won't happen again. I simply will not let it. He sleeps curled towards my chest, beside my heart. I keep her in her own room, with small bits by the doors and windows to protect her, or us from her. I'm not sure which. Sometimes I think that she could be my little one, my girl. She doesn't seem to mind the salt, the iron. The petals crushed in water in a bowl. These are good signs. All we can do is try to love her, and protect him fiercely.

A haon

When I was researching, reading up, I kept coming across all these little things that people do to tell the future. Tea leaves, apples, cards. It frightened me. I do not want to know. I need that little flame. The lick of hope. Her face is hers again when she's asleep, the little furrowed brow, the concentration. She has your chin, your mouth. But it's the light inside that worries me. That's where the difference is. That small, strange shift. And every parent messes something up, eventually. A matter of time. I plane my big hand over the round hotness of his baby stomach thrusting out, all full of love and milk. We can't take chances. And we can't afford to leave this place. What if she's somewhere hidden, looking for us? What if we're right? What if we're wrong?

A náid

Of course it hurts.
It hurts, and hurts, and hurts.

I BHFAD UAIM

The summer solstice is the turning point, when the sun shines longest, and after that the nights begin to stretch. A part of me always yearns for the darkness, even as I mourn the freedom of long evenings. I wanted to write a story about that journey, away from the light, towards something other, something that may feel uncertain. It was inspired by a story Oein shared with me, which his father told him, about a woman waiting with a lantern for her husband, long after he'd been lost.

———

The cottage was large, with thick white walls and a trellis that had once held dog roses but now just bare twigs, clinging, grey and skeletal. There were five rooms, apart from the bathroom – the skinny little kitchen, the large sitting room around the hearth where the open fire still held a little crane for hanging pots. The bedrooms, and the small room to the side, the one locked up. The house smelt clean, but not homely. People had been in and out of it, but just a weekend here, a weekend there. It hadn't been a home since Clíona died. Clíona was Sam's great-aunt, and she had lived alone in the cottage for most of her life. She had left it to Agnes, Sam's mother, out of love, and practicality. So she would always have a place to go.

Clíona had been a stout woman, with long gun-metal grey hair and sallow skin, particular and at times very cutting. Sam remembered her telling him he didn't have his sister's brains but he'd be grand regardless.

'I was only four,' he'd said to Holly. 'But I remembered it. How it upset me.'

Sam was quite easy-going generally, but he could be sensitive like that. Holly could never tell how something would hit him. It had driven her mad when they first got together. Still did, at times. But now she was sure he loved her back, and that he wouldn't leave her over something petty, which made things a lot less stressful. They'd been together for the past three years, and everybody knew that they were trying because he kept on saying it to people.

'You don't have to issue a statement,' Holly had told him.

'I'm not.' His face was flushed. 'I'm just excited. This is big.'

She'd put a hand on the cuff of his shirt, and smiled. 'Yeah. I suppose,' she said. 'Me too. Me too.'

Holly wasn't sure that she was ready, not like Sam was. She'd always thought there would be this moment when she had all of her shit together, a natural progression. It had happened that way for so many of her friends, but she would be forty on her next birthday, and if she didn't try now, there was the sense that it mightn't ever happen. She hadn't had any tests or her eggs counted or anything. It was just a feeling, not unlike in school when there was an exam that she'd meant to study for but hadn't. A sort of ache, between her ribcage and her navel. And Sam was really keen to be a dad. He'd always wanted it. He would be loads of help, he kept on saying, and Holly smiled and nodded as though she agreed, but she was thinking about how the baseline for a good dad was so much lower than it was for mothers. She already knew she wasn't going to be a good mother. She'd aim for adequate at best.

Holly had painted the set for a play that Sam had helped produce and that was how they'd met. He didn't do that professionally – he worked in tech – but his friend had written it and somehow he'd been roped in. Sam never admitted wanting to do anything. He'd fallen into a job in tech, fallen into loving her, and now they were falling into parenthood. I mean, it would happen for them. Probably. Sam wanted them to fall into Clíona's house, live there rent free. They'd have to do it up, but just a bit.

'Mam says it's ours,' he told her, 'if we want it.'

'Yeah, but it isn't ours, though. It's hers.' Holly felt her voice begin to rise, get shrill, she couldn't help it. 'Like, I don't want to be putting all of our savings into a place that won't belong to us.'

Sam's family had money, and he made more than Holly. He acted like he didn't even notice half the time, but it was harder to be blasé when she was the one contributing less. They drew up ground rules, but she had the sense that Sam would do exactly what he wanted anyway, and somehow it would work out for the best.

Clíona's cottage was beautiful. Sam's mother, Agnes, had it rented out most summers, and it had that vibe, pastel-striped, brushed-cotton bedsheets, magnolia walls. It had been kept up, but not made pretty. There were pictures hanging, little prints of lighthouses, and a photograph of the beach that Sam's Uncle Gerry had taken when he was making that coffee table book about the coastline. Sam's Uncle Gerry was kind of a big deal. He lived in New York. Agnes was always going on about him. Sam's family were close. Holly would like her potential baby to have that sort of loving, open family. Her crowd wasn't going to be like that, much and all as she cared for them. They made promises they meant to keep and didn't. Lost their tempers frequently and with relish. Holly's father was in a years-long feud with the council over bins. He had one room that he filled up with different colour-coded bin bags, which he ferried once a fortnight to the dump. In summer the smell of rubbish permeated everything, and if Holly mentioned it, she was accused of notions, starting fights. Sam's parents grew their own tomatoes and had a good relationship with their vintner, Lucas. It wasn't a contest, but if it was, he was winning.

And it made it harder, Sam's stability, the ease with which he moved through the world, the confidence. He felt this move was the right thing to do, and it probably was. He was better at life than Holly was. She had often said she'd like to move out to the country, but now that it was happening, she felt a sense of something close to panic. Out there, all they'd have would be each other. And space to create, of course. Holly had applied for a grant for a project based around folklore, the body and the landscape. On the basis that it would enable her to do exactly this. To move out to the cottage and have a swathe of time to do her thing. It had been sort of gig to gig until now. She'd made it work, paid her half of the rent, the bills. She hustled. That pressure being gone would be a dream. She just wasn't sure that it was one she wanted to come true. She closed her eyes and imagined life beside the waves, kept saying to herself that if she didn't get the bursary, they'd have to reconsider. It became a sort of waiting game, a little like the 'trying'. Holly tried not to think about it, or check her inbox too much. She bought conception vitamins and took them every day, and they had sex three times a week even when something really good had dropped on Netflix.

When the email arrived, Sam brought Champagne home, and it felt amazing. It did, that vote of confidence. That sense that she would be able to support herself. Have what her Auntie Laura called 'the running away fund'. Laura was big on everyone eventually leaving you high and dry. She'd been preparing Holly to be abandoned by a husband since childhood. Maybe that was why Holly was resistant to the idea of marrying. Sam would marry her in a heartbeat, she knew. But it would be so hard to ever end things then. Their lives were enmeshed as it was. It felt like any extra legal admin should be avoided. The thought of organising a big day was off-putting as well, the stress of it. But moving house wasn't that much better, and all of a sudden it was happening, they were boxing all their stuff up, labelling it. Some was going into the attic of his parents' garage, but most would fit in the cottage. He'd called some people in to do up an outhouse in the back, just enough that it could be her studio, and that made Holly's heart flip in a way she didn't really understand. It was so hard not to love Sam, really. Everything he did was fucking kind.

'You shouldn't have. It must have cost a fortune,' she said.

'Ah sure, all they did was put in some plugs, a lick of paint and an aul' door,' Sam said, and Holly smiled at him. It was more than that, and they both knew it.

Their last night in the flat, they slept on an air mattress they'd bought for guests when they had first moved in, and woke with the hardness of the floor against their backs.

"There must have been a hole in it or something," Sam said, and Holly nodded. They piled up the car with the last few bits the movers hadn't taken, and got two Americanos and some pastries for the drive.

'Are you okay?' Sam asked, an hour in. 'You've barely touched your cinnamon and walnut scroll.'

That was a thing he did, the exact naming of foods. Holly smiled across at him, bit into it. They turned some music on, a playlist that he'd made for their first road trip. The sun was shining, and it was so nice once they got out of city traffic. She kept on wanting to touch him in the sunlight. To stroke his hand on the gearstick. The sense of rightness that had been eluding her had arrived. It wouldn't stay, because hope had always been a fleeting sort of feeling for Holly, but for the moment it was lovely. Lovely.

She looked at the crinkle of his crow's feet, the slant of his smile, the shine of stubble on his face and wondered, *How am I here? How is this my life?* The skies were blue, and they stayed blue all the way to the cottage, through the flatlands and the hilly ones, past towns and shops and fields, and gardens, little snippets of wilderness and other people's lives.

When they arrived, the cottage was already full of boxes, but they decided not to bother with them just yet. Sam left her there and went to get a pizza and some beer, and Holly organised the box marked 'Kitchen One', and took three or four boxes of materials to her studio, left them there. She was putting their pyjamas under the pillows when she heard the footsteps moving in the kitchen. She called out to Sam that she'd be there in a minute and smoothed down the bedspread. It was cream with little sprigs of lavender embroidered on the bottom. Very Agnes. They'd need to paint this room, and probably buy a dehumidifier, and the garden out the window needed tending. The grass was looking shaggy. Sam's family did an indoor-outdoor Easter egg hunt every year. His father, Colm, wrote clues, sometimes in multiple languages, and everyone had to find their Easter egg. Last year, her one had been in the guest bathroom, perched beside the shampoo on the little shower rack. She'd smiled along, but it dragged on a bit. Nice for the children though. If they had a baby, then it would be a bit different, maybe. She called to Sam again – the pizza would get cold if she didn't hurry – and was startled by the rumble of his car pulling into the yard. Holly felt the panic start to build. She waited in the room to hear his voice, wondering if she should shout out to warn him, what could happen.

Sam's voice rang out through the house, calling Holly's name, and she went to him, self-consciously brandishing an ornamental jug. He was blithely gathering napkins and glasses and there was no sign that anyone had been here, as far as she could tell. She smiled at him, and went to put the jug back, checked each room, pressing her ear to the door of the locked one. There was nothing to arouse suspicion. She ate her pizza, smiled, and didn't tell Sam she was on edge. There was no point ruining a lovely day. It had felt so real though. She had been sure that there was someone there.

They went to bed with full stomachs. When she woke, she felt the warmth of Sam against her back and turned towards him. The ghost of toothpaste lingered on his tongue, and the sunlight was pouring through the small gap in the curtains. They had the kind of sex they used to have. Holly felt full, and part of her thought that it would be nice if their baby came from that feeling, the warmth and love and rightness of them both, no gritted teeth and schedules. Sam went to make her coffee and she stretched her legs and arms out as though she were making snow angels in the sheets. The steps last night seemed very far away, and the day was full of promise. They made breakfast, walked up the road and over to the beach and stared out at the boats, looking for seals because Agnes had said that sometimes they swam by.

'Clíona must have stood here,' Sam said, pointing to the dunes, the rocks, 'when she was waiting for him to come home.'

Clíona had been married to a man called Muirt. Muirt had been tall, and brave, and fond of laughter. The story went that he had courted her for a full two years before she agreed to marry him. Not because she didn't love him but because she wanted to be full sure he loved her enough to keep on trying. They had been married in the small white-washed chapel in the village, and for ten years life had been as they planned. They had been happy, or as close as people get to happy, Agnes had told Sam, who told Holly.

And she had asked him, 'How did people know that it was real, the happiness?'

He'd shrugged, and told her he'd never thought to ask. Maybe it was that they took care of each other. They kept each other warm. People used to remark on the way that Clíona went down to the beach with her lantern held high and a little flask of tea for him to drink to get the warmth of home back in his bones after a long time out at sea. He didn't want to be a fisherman for ever, but it was what he knew and so he kept on going with it, and they planned their future. Clíona took a bit of sewing in, but the little room she worked in was always supposed to be for someone small who'd come from both of them. And they had time, or thought that they had time.

Agnes had never met her Uncle Muirt, but she had grown up missing him. There was a storm, and there was a boat with two young lads out there. Muirt went to help and the two boys came back but he did not. They never found the body. Clíona couldn't believe it, not in the dull strange way that loss can hit a person. She simply did not accept that Muirt was dead. He would come home to her. He always had before, and so she waited.

Holly looked up at the sand dune, imagining what it would be if Sam just disappeared, a blank space there. She'd had her heart broken three times before she met him. And each of them had felt a little different, in the way that storms are different. She looked out at the waves. They were the same grey as the sky and she could see the ripple of the mountains across the water, just the soft blur of them. She must have made a sound. Sam stroked her arm, asked if she was okay.

'Yeah, just thinking.'

'About Clíona?'

'Yeah,' she said again and took his hand.

When they got back, they put the kettle on, made a list of jobs and a list for shopping, drove to the nearest Lidl and stocked up. They were going to do it room by room. Beginning with the smallest one, where Clíona had done her sewing. It was locked and had been used for storage before that. The door had been painted over and they couldn't even open it with the key. They could make it into a little office space for Sam, but they were going to do it in a way that meant it could also be a spare room for visitors and a possible nursery. Lots of organising, lots of plans. Holly traced her fingers over the door of the small room, and wondered. Sam said it was probably full of mice and dust, but she was dying to have a nose. The door was a question mark. And once it opened, it would just become a list of jobs. A bit like with the baby, if they had one. She rubbed her stomach, and Sam asked if she wanted a cup of tea.

That evening, Holly did a batch cook on the cute seventies cooker that looked neat as a pin. There was a local woman, Sara, who Agnes paid to come in and clean once a week. She must be good; the place was sparkling clean. Agnes had begged them to keep her on.

'I won't say much,' she told them, 'But there's a very sad story there.'

Holly felt a little weird about having a cleaner at all. But if it was the kind thing to do, then they should do it, and it freed her up to work on the art, the house, at least a little. There was still so much work to be done.

The next day, Sam was working from eight a.m. and she did a bit of yoga in the garden. There was a little push lawnmower in the corner of her studio, and after work, she'd have to cut the grass. She looked over at the other space behind it, through a gate, and that had been let wild. Holly wasn't even sure whether to call it a garden or a field. It was something in between. A patch, perhaps. They weren't sure if they should start growing their own vegetables or leave it for the bees. There were rhododendrons in the fields across the way. They grew wild here, not as plentiful as gorse, but holding their own. The bright pink shock of them. She'd always liked rhododendrons. They reminded her of her nan's garden when she was a child. Nan was long dead now, but the memory of her was still a place where Holly felt so safe. She'd loved routine. Breakfast at seven, dinner at twelve, tea at five, bed at half past eight. They could have their own little routine here, Holly thought. A slower pace. In Dublin, there was always a reason to be busy, and here they would be working hard, but in a different way. At this early stage, it was hard to tell if that was good or bad. But she had hope. The door was painted shut, but it would open.

She tidied the kitchen and went into her studio for a few hours, reading and sketching, and looking up the different seaweeds that she remembered from the beach. At lunchtime she made an omelette for Sam and brought it in. It was light and fluffy, and round like the sun, and the light was filtering through the windows. He kissed her on the cheek and his eyes were very blue and glad to see her. This cottage was a place disposed to happiness, she thought. Disposed to love. Hungry for it, even. When she went back to the kitchen to wash up, the water had been switched on already, even though she didn't recall doing it, and she looked out at the gate.

Some people like their kitchen windows to face the garden, but the kitchen faced the road, so Holly could always see who was coming by. She thought of Clíona's lantern again, as her eyes travelled the length of it, the line of soft grass pushing through the tarmac. It was bright now, but when the darkness came, it would be darker than in the city, even with the canopy of stars. The other houses on this road seemed newer, so it must have been darker again when Clíona was out there shining her light, on her lonely way up to the beach. What Agnes called 'a proper, country dark'. Sam had just a few memories of Clíona; she passed away when he was only five. Still walking down the road to the beach every night, holding her lantern high. Still waiting, for an hour and sometimes more, for Muirt to come home to her. And everyone telling her to mind herself, and that she should be careful on the road, it had no footpath yet, no lights and, of course, people absolutely bombed it, and she would nod, and smile, and do exactly what she wanted to do. Holly pictured her, walking in the gate. She'd worn a floral blouse, a calf-length skirt in the picture Agnes had shown her, taken at Sam's christening. Holly wondered how old she had been when she got married. And what it would be like, one golden omelette day, to marry Sam. She shook her head and smiled, and went back to the studio. The light was good, and she could see a little scrape of hill from the window. The lambs were in the fields, but all that she could make out at this distance were white dots of different sizes. Tomorrow, she would go for a long walk, or a drive maybe.

There was a knock on the door. She looked down at the time, it was getting late, and she wanted to get a start on that small room. She stood up, apologising, and opened the door. Whoever had been there was already gone, but the back door was open and she went in, calling Sam's name.

He came out of the nook behind a screen where he had set up the computer, and looked at her apologetically.

'Have you been calling long?' He tapped his headphones. 'I'm sorry.'

Holly shook her head. 'No, you knocked on my door . . . and then the back was open. I assumed . . .'

A look of worry passed over Sam's face. 'I probably left it open when I emptied the bins earlier. I'd need to watch that or we could get mice.'

Holly smiled. She oddly quite liked mice. Obviously she understood the need to not have them in the cupboards, but they were so nicely shaped and tiny and complete.

Sam's eyes narrowed. 'Did you leave the door open yourself in search of mice, Holly? Don't lie to me.' He waggled his fingers, threatening to tickle her. Their eyes met and they laughed and it was good. Holly looked back at the door and it was closed. But it had been open. Someone had knocked. She'd heard those feet. She shivered.

'Maybe we should get a locksmith for the door.'

'Bit of a segue.' Sam tilted his head that way he did, performing his perplexity.

'Yeah.' She looked away, out through the window.

'Where did you go just there?' Sam asked. 'You were off thinking about something.'

'I was, yeah. Just, like, if you didn't knock, who did? That kind of thing.'

'I'll have a look around,' he said, 'take the big stick.'

Holly smiled, but he did take the stick, a long blackthorn one with a twisted knobby handle, and then she felt a good deal less like smiling. She suddenly thought of Clíona, walking the road down to the sea alone. Holding her lantern, and later on, her torch. Just step by step. That was something Holly would never do, walk alone at night in a place where nobody would hear her if she called out for help.

'Mum is bringing us over dinner this evening,' Sam said, tilting his head back around the half door. 'She just texted me there.'

Holly sighed. 'There's no need, like. We have plenty of food. I do like cooking.'

'So do I, but she wanted to. A welcome. I couldn't really tell her no.' He shrugged.

He widened his eyes, and Holly thought about before, at home, when she'd told him this house would come with strings. Better not to stir it; he looked tired. She shook her head.

'No, no, it's fine. It's fine. I mean, she'll probably want to stay and eat with us as well?'

Sam nodded.

Agnes swept in about an hour later, with a bottle of 'the most gorgeous Chilean red' with a leaf on the front of it and a tub of home-made granola, as well as the lasagne and various salads.

'A feast!' Holly exclaimed, intent on masking how annoyed she was at not having the time and space with Sam. Her eyes drifted over to the little room as she arranged the cutlery on either side of the table mats and placed the water glasses just so, the way that Agnes did when they were over. Agnes always said she took people as she found them, but Holly didn't fancy testing her on that.

'Are there any photographs of Clíona, like from when she was young, of her and Muirt maybe?' Holly asked. 'It might be nice to put one up, to honour the history, like.'

'Oh, that's a lovely idea.' Agnes smiled. 'I know Gerry went through everything and made a digital archive several years ago. For an exhibition.'

'I think it's a great idea,' Sam said. 'You know, I've been thinking of her so much since we moved in.'

'Me too,' Holly said. 'I mean, I never met her. But there's a sense of something special in the house.'

Agnes nodded. 'This is why people kept on asking to come back summer after summer.'

'What was she like?' Holly asked.

'I don't know is the answer,' Agnes said. 'I feel like there was a bit of a shell to her. She used to wash the bodies, get them ready before funerals. And we used to say that she was only doing it so they would take her messages to Muirt, over in the land of the dead.' She smiled. 'Very pagan of us. You'd approve, Holly.'

Holly took a bite of her salad. It was, unsurprisingly, excellent. She made a sound halfway between enjoyment and agreement.

Sam took a slice of pain de campagne from the basket in the middle of the table. 'No more wine for you, Mum. You'll have us believing in ghosts.'

'Ah, it was only a small glass. I am driving though, so I'll be good. Sara's keeping hens now, selling eggs. I've put you down for two dozen a week.'

Holly swallowed. 'I'll have to start baking.'

'Or having people over.' Agnes raised an eyebrow.

'We're only here three days,' Sam said. 'We need time to get settled.'

Agnes inclined her head and touched the delicate graphic brooch on her lapel.

Holly looked at Sam's expression, absolutely neutral. He met her eye, and she almost giggled, but turned it into a cough.

'Is something funny?' Agnes said.

Holly took another slug of wine and looked over at the space on the wall where she'd thought they could put the picture of Clíona and Muirt. It was as though she could remember something hanging there.

'A Sacred Heart,' she said. 'There used to be a Sacred Heart up there.'

They looked at her.

'You're right, Holly,' Agnes said. 'There was a Sacred Heart up there when Clíona lived here. I took it down. I wanted to put something else up instead. That wall always looked a little blank. But everything I put up just fell down. It was' – she crossed her cutlery across the plate – 'a little spooky.'

'Wow,' said Sam. 'You never told me that.'

'Oh you were very young, pet. You probably just don't remember.' She looked across the fold-out table, at Holly. 'It didn't scare me. I've always felt very safe here, in this house. I think that was Clíona's intention when she passed it on to me. She never liked your father.'

'Oh,' said Sam.

'Luckily I like him very much,' said Agnes, with a grin. 'I just don't think that any man could measure up to what she had with Muirt. And I wondered if the time, the distance, had sort of made her heart grow fonder. But she would talk about him all the time, little things, like how he'd leave the back door open for her when she was coming back from the garden. How he had more time for songs about love than songs about rebellion, and how he had his own recipe for soda bread, that his mother taught him, and she could never get it to taste exactly right once he was gone. She never called him dead, you know. There was always this sense that he'd come back again. His things were kept in place, the house was ready . . .'

'Creepy,' Sam said.

'Lovely,' Agnes said. 'Imagine. A love that lasts that long, with nothing back. No sign, no sight, no warmth.'

'It's valiant,' Holly said. 'It's valiant. To keep that light, that call to him. That welcome.'

'Yes. Valiant. Exactly. When my mother died, I felt her very close to me in the beginning. Like she was still in rooms that I was in. I could almost feel her brushing my hair. And there were little things, you know, like signs. A butterfly. A robin. A small white feather for me on the path. Finding a birthday card she'd written for Sam while I was clearing out her house.'

'I still have that,' Sam said, with a fond grin.

'Of course you do, my love.' She reached across the table, squeezed his hand. 'But . . . once she'd been gone for a while, I found myself a little chilled by those things, those signals. There was a sense that she wasn't where she was supposed to be. I felt on edge, humming with the worry, like when she was sick. The cat brought home a robin in its mouth, my hair in tangles, everything felt like it was an omen. One day, there was this butterfly, this yellow butterfly, and something must have caught it, and it was there on the windowsill struggling to fly, working and working at its wings when one of them had crumpled, and I went into the cupboard and got a candle, and I just said, "Mummy I love you,

I do, I really do. And I know that you love me. It's time to be at peace." I opened the window, Holly. And . . . it flew out. And after that, I couldn't feel her out there any more, just in my heart where she was supposed to be. I don't know.' Agnes sighed. 'Maybe there's a time to let things go.

Holly thought of the Sacred Heart picture in her nan's house, the votive underneath it, protecting everyone. They left it in the house when it had been sold on. That money was long gone now. She got up to refill the water jug, turned on the tap, and for a moment heard the sound of water rushing in her ears, felt something pulling her under, under, under. It was a gentle pull, she could still breathe, even through the strange sensation. The water running over her hands jarred her out of it. The jug was full.

When she returned, Agnes was standing.

'It's time I took my leave of you,' she said, smoothing down her linen trousers, 'thank you both for such a lovely evening. I feel lighter.'

'Drive safe, Mum.' Sam said. 'I love you.' He kissed her on the cheek and Holly murmured her goodbyes as well, mildly astonished at the way that families could say those things so easily. She knew that she was loved, she was. But they didn't go around saying it to each other.

She traced her hand over the wall. She could feel the bumps and ridges of the stone beneath the layers and layers of shiny paint. And she thought of how easy it was, to click into this routine. How smooth and safe it felt. And felt the rush of water in her ears, and muffled worlds, something like shocking.

Seachain.

Beware, she thought. Sam wrapped his arms around her waist and she snuggled into him. He wanted to leave the clear-up but she couldn't go to sleep with dirty dishes, so they got on with it together. Sam placed the plates on the drying rack, and while she was thinking about how much she missed the dishwasher, he approached and put his arms around her. Tenderly, but with a strength as well, a hint of power that she wasn't used to. Something in her tightened and relaxed. Her head against his chest, she listened to the thump thump of his heart. It was going very fast and his hands were at the small of her back and his mouth was on hers and she was drowning, drowning. She clung to the rough wool of his jumper, and suddenly they were in the bed and she had no idea how they got from one place to another, they just were and she wasn't thinking with her brain at all but just seeking sensation, he was on her, in her, and she could feel the heat of him, the pulse. It was like they weren't two different people at all, but two halves of the one thing. Clawing, grinding, desperate to get home.

Holly woke the next morning, and Sam was looking at her from the pillow. She smiled and trailed a finger out. He flinched, and something puckered in her heart.

'What is it, love?' she said.

'I don't know.' He swallowed. 'I feel. Last night . . . I didn't have that much to drink but when we . . . it felt like I did. It felt weird. Like I was here, but also not. Or something.'

Holly moved a little bit away. Her stomach clenched.

'Oh,' she said. 'I didn't realise. I mean . . .' Her voice was high, defensive.

'No, no. I'm not saying you did anything wrong, you didn't. I'm just being weird.'

Sam brushed at the sheets and didn't meet her eye. Holly thought of the water rushing in her ears, the sound of muffled shouting, worry, warning.

'Did we use . . . ?' he asked.

'No,' she said. 'We're trying. Remember?'

Sam sat up. 'I know. I know we're trying. It's just.' He closed his eyes. 'I didn't feel like me.'

'What, like you felt . . . possessed?' Holly tried to keep her voice as neutral as possible and pulled the sheets around her body. They were both naked and neither of them wanted to be, now.

'No . . . it was . . . like do you know when you get pins and needles in your leg and it kind of takes the leg a while to remember it's part of your body? It was like, like that. Like my brain was asleep. And I was aware of everything that happened but I was very far away as well, and looking down from there.' He pointed to the corner of the ceiling, at a small discoloured patch of damp. A water stain.

'Oh God,' Holly said. 'Oh God. I'm sorry.'

Sam took her in his arms. 'How could you know?'

'I knew that there was something different. I felt it, but I thought it was the both of us together, not me experiencing one thing and you going through something else.'

There was the sound of feet outside. And they both heard it this time, and they looked at each other. Sam got up, pulled on his boxer shorts, and left the room. She got pyjama bottoms and a T-shirt, the thought of him not wanting it humming through her, sick. Not right, not right. There was something in this house with them, and it had made her hurt him without meaning to. All of a sudden he felt far away, and she had the strongest urge to see his face again, to have him smile at her. She staggered out of bed and after Sam, but when she reached the sitting room she stopped. The door that had been sealed was hanging open.

'Sam?' she said.

And higher, louder, 'Sam?'

The cottage was so silent. She felt cold, as if it weren't spring but close to winter. As if the air outside were rushing through. She walked towards it, feeling something curling in. The first time Sam had asked her to marry him, he had been really sure she would say yes. He'd taken her out to their favourite restaurant and asked her over dessert. Banoffee pie. There had been a bottle of Champagne waiting behind the bar, and when she'd turned him down, he had asked her to nod and drink it anyway. The staff were looking. He would be embarrassed. But she hadn't. She didn't want to live in someone else's story. In a lie. And she knew how much that had hurt him, because he had been abrupt with her for days, and then just sad. He'd told her once he wished he could be sure of her. She had smiled and brushed it off, but she knew what he meant.

Inside, the room was bigger than she'd thought it would be, and there were bolts of fabric on the shelves, and a dress form in the corner with a gingham jacket half-assembled on it. A crinkled pattern laid out on the table. On the wall there was a black and white wedding photo of two people. The woman in a little tailored suit, a pillbox hat. The man tall and imposing in his dress suit. It would be blue or brown, she thought. Black was for funerals, she'd heard that somewhere. They weren't smiling widely, but they were kind of shining with each other. Like a beacon, brightening the room. The shutters were closed, and it should have been dim there but it wasn't, she could see it all. And there was not a single speck of dust. It was just there. She trailed her finger over the opened page of a magazine, and looked to make sure it wasn't a trick of the light. And it was shining, shining, sort of beckoning. *Come home, come home. Come home, I've kept it perfect. Come home, my love. I've journeyed for so long.*

Holly felt the desire to sit at the table and take up the work rising in her. And she could, they could be happy here. Sam and she. Could marry, have a baby. She planed her hand against the curve of her stomach. There could even be one already in her, growing. All she had to do was reach out for it, take it. It would be hers, and all whatever still lived in this house would ask was just a little taste. A little warmth every now and then, and she could work late in her studio and find the kettle boiled when she came back, and they could make new memories, new joys here. Find peace.

Seachain, though.

Holly swallowed, and she closed her eyes. It wouldn't be her life.

The happiness, it wouldn't be just hers. She felt a reassuring hand on her shoulder, and if she closed her eyes and breathed it in, she knew it could be Sam, it could be comfort, but she turned around, and nobody was there. She went to the window and looked out. The view was beautiful, but she could almost see the light leeching away, all but one little speck, calling, calling her in from the cold. In from the loneliness. From . . . what had Agnes called it, just last night?

The land of the dead.

Not heaven or hell, but just another place. And it would take a long time for a message to travel there, and longer still for someone to make the journey, step by desperate step back to the hungry heart that waited for them. Years and years, perhaps. And what if when he got there, it was too late, and Clíona had gone to join him, but she couldn't now. Because he wasn't there. He had come home. So all that he could do was love and long, and wait and keep on loving and longing and waiting, until that was all of him that still remained. The water rushing up around his ears, and love, and love, and love and love and love.

Holly held a hand to her cheek and realised that she was sobbing, choking on her grief, not only for Muirt and Clíona, but for this thing, this hardness in her that still resisted all the gentleness and joy that was around her. That wasn't ready to shine, for Sam, or even for herself. This promised happiness, it wouldn't be theirs, not really. It would not be something they had built or earned or won. It would all be too easy to give in and let this place unfold, this life unfurl. And she had never been the kind of person who could do that. Who could let things lie. She couldn't just be grateful for a meal, a home, a heart. She had to look for flaws. She had to find them. And she had to leave. She had to leave.

Holly closed her eyes and keened, that was the only word for it, the sound of loss that felt carved out of her. Sam's eyes, Sam's face. His hand upon her back. His smile. His smile. She hadn't earned it, any of it, he had just kept on giving and giving and giving and she hadn't meant to but she had taken something from him now. And she could not undo it. Even if . . . if things . . . if it were different.

Seachain.

The world was what it was. Holly opened her eyes, and Sam was there beside her in the room, and it was full of dust and dirt and cobwebs. And when she opened her mouth, she knew that it would be the start of an ending, and so she sat, and stared, and didn't speak, eyes moving, searching, for a guide, a little beam of light that wasn't there for her, if it was there.

ACKNOWLEDGEMENTS

Stories come from people. Those we know and those we do not know. I'm hugely grateful to Fionnuala, Gráinne and Nidhi of Skein Press for their vision for this book and their support and insight as it developed, and to Éilís for her intricate and beautiful bookbinding. I'd also like to thank Chandrika and Cormac for their work getting it to readers, and Robert for his keen observations during the proofreading process.

Stories come from places. I'm so thankful to the Tyrone Guthrie Centre at Annaghmakerrig for giving us space away from the world to connect with this project and with each other.

Stories come from friends. To Oein and Yingge, it is a privilege to know you both. I'm so glad our work was able to weave together. Connection and creativity are such powerful gifts. I'd also like to thank my friend Louise, who read a draft of 'Lao Mara' and provided me with compassionate and expert feedback.

Stories come from allies. Thank you to my agents, Clare Wallace and Chloe Davis. I'm so grateful to have you in my corner.

Stories come from gifts. Thank you to Owenie DeBhairduin, Oein's father, who shared with him a tale he shared with me, that inspired 'I bhFad Uaim'. It's no small thing to be trusted with a story. I hope I did it justice. I'd also like to thank Eddie Lenihan, whose stories I first encountered as a child looking up in awe in Sheela-Na-Gig Bookshop in Galway, and whose podcast kept me company on long drives and buggy walks as this book was crafted. The National Folklore Collection at UCD is a gift indeed. Their podcast and online collection was such a rich source of knowledge as I developed my connection to and understanding of the wheel of the year and the wealth of tradition and story connected with it. I would also like to thank the Arts Council for their support, and the gift of time.

Stories come from love. To my extended family, for reaching your arms around me even when we couldn't touch each other. To Nana for stories, songs and always, always love. And finally, to Diarmuid and Bonnie, for making joy so easy to find, even when the nights stretch long in front of us. Thank you for your patience and jiggy little legs, respectively.

WEAVE

WEAVE

OEIN DEBHAIRDUIN

skein press

First published in 2022 by Skein Press
www.skeinpress.com

Cover design and layout by Éilís Murphy of Folded Leaf
Illustrations by Yingge Xu of The Art of the Brush
Printed by Walsh Colour Print, Co. Kerry, Ireland

A CIP catalogue for this title is available from the British Library.

ISBN 978-1-9164935-7-5

Skein Press gratefully acknowledges the financial support it receives from the
Arts Council of Ireland.

Skein Press are also grateful to Dublin UNESCO City of Literature and Dublin
City Council for their support.

These offerings are dedicated to the women in my life who have helped mould me, who have minded me, carried me and been a torch in the dark, even when they too were wandering in the twilight.

To Catherine, to Teresa, to Kathleen, to Trina, to Tashes Kayk, to Eileen, to Maggie, to Mary. You have been my foundation, my compass, my backbone and the whisperers of the muni tober.

CONTENTS

C
A
R
M
A
N

As the high sun of summer begins to welcome the growing coolness of autumn, Lúnasa, the first harvest, takes place with the claiming of the wheat and oats, the cleaving of the stalks and the reaping of the grains. It is a time not only to remember the efforts of the past that have brought so much bounty into our lives but also one of celebration.

I have always enjoyed the rituals of the changing seasons, be it the building of the bonfires or the visits to local parishes on high market days. There is something so potent and powerful in communal understandings of the change in the world around us and how we as people also change in reaction to that growth. As time passes in its ever-moving circle, I have come to realise that my favourite season is usually the one I am currently in.

This tale of Carman was first told to me by a neighbour, Mick, who shared it with me as we stood, arms crossed and leaning on his wrought-iron gate, watching the world go by from among the blossoming delights of his garden. Like the festivals held throughout the year, such as Tlachtga, Raigne and the Tailteann games, the festival of Carman was held every three years, both in memory of she who led an invasion and in celebration of the prosperity that returned.

Those who had the eyes, who could see, noticed the signs long before her arrival. The ewes of the field had brought no lambs that spring while the salmon refused to leap upstream. Instead of reaching towards the light and warmth of the sun, the shafts of grain leaned away from the waters of the sea. The apples grew slight and paltry on the trees.

She had many names, as many as the shades of fear she struck into the hearts of all who witnessed her, but the one she was known as most of all was Carman.

Carman was a warrior of blade and battlefield, of wit and war and death and destruction. She was also a woman of the other ways, a worker of magic and enchantment, of secrets spun in the night and curses spoken in the midday sun. Those on land who saw the arrival caught a glimpse of the tall, strong woman whose hair whipped in the wind, as long as the sails were wide, and whose shoulders stood just above the boom of the gale-weathered vessel. She did not come alone. She arrived with three men, each one her son, whose names and titles carried with them the mark they would leave upon the world.

There was Dubh, named for darkness, who was tall and wide and went in slow movements, creeping through the rooms and fields he travelled like a shadow at dusk. Dothar, monikered for evil, was small and gaunt, with features as sharp as his tongue. And Dian, Dian with his wild hair and darting eyes, was named of violence.

Trouble followed the four swifter than the bark of a maddened dog down a lonely road as they crossed the lands of Éire. The people of that ancient island and those who stood in kinship and care of it, known as the Tuatha Dé Danann, grew more and more concerned at the claiming of the land for which they themselves had undertaken long bloody battles.

Carman began to enchant the soil when local clans would not offer her tribute or bow their heads low in honour of her. With each step of her feet, she ensured that rot and ruin was entwined in every root and growth in the earth. Fruit withered on the vine, flower buds once near to bursting with bright blossoms grew crusty brown and hollow. Even the bread in the ovens refused to rise and turned quickly to mould.

As he travelled, Dubh would reach up and out, coiling his grime-encrusted fingers into the air to draw down heavy clouds that would dim the day as if it was the depth of night, bringing great heaviness and tense melancholy.

Dothar would wander and shuffle around, mumbling words and phrases. The sound was never understood by those whose ears it visited, but within a day those same people would become pale and red-eyed, with heads and hearts deep in the grind of suspicion and anger, any goodness toward their neighbour siphoned off, leaving them ready to reply to any kindness with the sharpest of tongues.

Dian too held his brutal sway. With his comings and goings the natural flow of life was disturbed and made malignant. Owls rarely screeched or took wing to the sky and even the bees of the fields took to mayhem and brought no honey, and so no mead was made.

Famine had truly begun to edge its way into Ireland, not only the famine that claimed the food of families but the one that starved them of kindness, warmth and open hearts. The geese of the low lands refused flight, and those who depended on fresh meat went without, and the comfort of friends became a rarity when the blunt impact of knuckles rather than the exchange of kind words became the greeting.

Finally the Tuatha Dé Danann took action against the scourge of Carman and her three sons. They swiftly decided that they would not, and could not, allow the destruction to continue, so they gathered and assembled four of their own people to stand in challenge against them.

From the north came Bé Chuille, druidess and worker of the soil, keeper of peace as well as a farm. Her name stood well in the calls of honour, as she had once invoked the aid of the stones from the low grounds and the trees of the field sides and they shot themselves arrows, to drive back an invading army.

Next they summoned Lugh, son of Cachar, from the east, who was a magician, who drew upon the stars for insights, direction and charm. He could make star maps for safe travels from the Irish waters to the cold lands of the north.

The match not yet made, next they called out for Aí from the west, son of Ollamh, whose poetic words carried such strength that one man, upon hearing them, could have the power and stamina of four.

Then came Crichibhéal from the south, who heard word of the gathering defence against Carman and her sons three. Crichibhéal was a bard and satirist whose songs and sayings could cause such shame to people that they would be stuck to the spot and hot weeping welts would rise up on their faces.

The match was made – four for four.

It took weeks for the warriors of the Tuatha Dé Danann to find Carman and her sons. It was only upon seeing the blight in a place that the four could know they had been there. They travelled and tracked them, always a step behind. Finally, a thought rose in Bé Chuille; instead of seeking out the wounded land, they would find them more readily amongst the green grasses that had yet to be torn asunder.

Finally, one dark night, their paths crossed in the midlands.

Carman, on seeing them approach, from a far hill, quickly cursed the weapons of the four warriors so that their swords would be dull and heavy. Bé Chuille, on noticing the bluntness of her dagger and seeing the small figure of Carman in the distance, quickly understood the sorcery. Unfazed and with a calm hand, she took stones from a lakeside and with ease took to grinding and polishing the blade back to a gleaming sharpness.

Dubh, who stood beside his mother, raised up his arms and grew loud with words of spite and fire, turning the sky stormy so that strikes of lightening would come slicing down upon the warriors. Lugh ran towards the hill on which Dubh posed, his own hands outstretched far up into the sky, calling for the stars to burn all the brighter, until their glow and light pierced through the storm-raged clouds of Dubh's wickedness and the sky was clear and calm.

Dothar, on Carman's other side, called out words of distraction and confusion to those who had come to challenge them, so that they could hardly pace forward in a straight line and looked at each other in bewilderment and rage until they had all but lost their senses and forgot their reason for being there. All but Aí, who remained unaffected by bitter words, began to see enemies in the faces of their friends. Before they could cut flesh from bone, Aí sung out words of honeyed sweetness so that the forgetfulness was shook from them and they once again knew each other and the task that lay before them.

The four warriors and invaders drew closer to each other, from hill to lakeside, and the battle was finally about to commence. Before the clattering of metal, pounding of shields and the spitting of harm could begin, Dian, moving in front of his mother and brothers, fixed his eyes sternly on the heroes. His gaze was as piercing as the tip of the dagger in his hand, and they felt a great weakness pour over them like a murky winter water that threatened to snuff out their spirits. The warriors were filled with the urge to cast aside their shields and weapons, so that they would be left unprotected from the invaders. Crichibhéal, holding on to the last threads of his strength, sung out a song of shame upon the invaders, so bitter the words and mortifying the call that they could not move but were stuck still and began to twist within themselves, until they each fell to their knees, swivelling in the up-trodden soil in utter agony.

At last, they were defeated.

The warriors were still noble, however, and did not wish to slay enemies who had already suffered the shame of their defeat, which would haunt their days. So they set about them a binding choice, a life-claiming oath. The three sons could leave but Carman would remain as hostage. If ever the sons returned, the heroes could claim her life's blood. That, or all four would now be cleaved from this life.

The three brothers chose banishment and their mother was chained to the barren walls of a cave, deep beneath the earth so that her workings would never be felt upon the land again.

With the sons banished and Carman imprisoned, the blight that had been set upon the crops lifted, and once again the harvests were a celebration of bounty.

Carman's final breath left her body, and her life was no more. So tormented was she by her defeat at the hands of the warriors and by her children's abandonment that her spectre was forever bound to Ireland and could not leave. However, her soul was not allowed on Irish soil due to the crimes she had inflicted upon that land, so she was forced to travel the rivers, streams and lakes for eternity, looking upon the world she once sought to claim as her own. Even the Aos Sí shunned her and from that day on refused to cross water so they would never grace her with their presence.

To this day and perhaps to the many days to come, when harvesting time is near, and before the first crop is claimed, some still say they see a glimpse of Carman upon the waters, where she waits in want of soil and sons.

S
L
I
A
B
H

N
A

M
B
A
N

September is the time of the second harvest. After the claiming of the grain, comes the digging for the roots. That which is beneath the surface often holds many surprises. The magic of seeds, once sowed in the moist darkness, growing to life, is a wonder. In times long past, before we had the scholars of science, people believed this to be an enchantment. This abiding mystery would often draw people's minds to places distant and stranger than those which can be seen and stepped upon. The claiming of this earthy bounty is not only a time of hearty feed but a reflection of our own often forgotten roots. The tendrils of the past connect and ground us not only to the present but in very real, meaningful ways to place and people. Traditionally people feared a woman who survived in the world without a man, be it unmarried or in widowhood. She was seen as peculiar, in possession of some power that was sustaining. This force was seen to be all the more darksome if she held it over another woman.

This tale came into my life at a storytelling event in Killorglin, during one of the family visits to the markets. My father, on a rare occasion in a public house, had me squirrelled away in a corner, while a woman, no taller than the fireplace she stood beside, told the story of the women of Slievenamon. Her name was Nora and her people knew mine and mine knew hers. Her mother, also a storyteller and a keeper of words, was a Traveller, and her father a country-man, and she a full person onto herself. She moved and whirled with the tale, enacting the story as she went. It may have been the very first time I witnessed a story being shared not just as an exchange of thought and wonder but as an enchanting performance.

Srani sat beside her high-stacked fire. The glow and warmth of it was a great comfort against the starkness of the deep night. She was the only one awake, for her beloved children and husband were sleeping in their beds. They had lived in the little cottage at the foothills of Slievenamon for as many years as she had fingers on her hard-working hands. The cottage had long been abandoned, with rumours abound that all those who lived there were visited by the witches of the mountain. Srani and her family had found it a small, squat, mouldy homestead and turned it into an inviting home of warmth and shared care.

The calm of the night was disturbed by loud knocks and kicks upon the door. Srani swiftly rose to open it, thinking that such a clamour could only come from a neighbour in need. As soon as the door had been unlatched, a woman, small and squat, pushed in and took a leap to the fireside, barking out, 'I am the witch of the one horn!'

Srani saw a horn on the temple of the uninvited visitor, short and curled, twisting out from just beneath her hair and reaching down as far as her ear. It looked like the branch of an old tree and was tight and dry like withered bone.

The woman sat beside the fire, squatting so that her knees were higher than her shoulders. She took from under her cloak a drop spindle and began to weave some cord, light blue like a midday spring sky.

Confused by the sight of the intruder, Srani stood there looking at the witch, her gaze only broken by another loud knock and bashing at the door. Again she turned to open it and in rushed another woman, this time carrying with her a spinning wheel beneath her arm. She too shouted out a shrill calling: 'I am the witch of the two horns!' Turning her head to show the twig-like horns, one upon her temple and the other between her two bushy eyebrows, she sat by the first.

Soon more clattering and clamouring was heard at the door. One after another came more witches, so that soon Srani found her room filled with twelve in all. Some were tall and sharply thin, with hair that hung in lank strands in front of their faces. Others were small and round and wore garments of brown, with high-held hoods so that only their mouths could be seen. Each one who arrived had a one more horn then the witch before. Some were spread out like a crown upon their heads, having torn through the hoods; others were bundled, like tightly bound rhubarbs, just above their ears.

Soon all the witches were spinning and weaving, cording and carding, making a great amount of noise, and the room filled up with their creations. Blankets began to spread across the floor, cords dropped over each chair and table, rovings were dashed on each window and skeins hung on door handles and lined the skirting boards.

Srani became upset at the sight and sound of it all, but as she began to object, one of the witches snapped her fingers and as soon as the sound was heard, no words could leave Srani's lips. Another clapped her hands in front of Srani and she was unable to move. A spell had been placed upon her, which ran through her bones and veins like the deep frost of a winter's night, striking her stiff and solid, unable to move even a finger or give blink to her eye. Fear hung heavy upon her, but heaviest of all was the worry for her family.

Eventually the witches grew tired from all their work and hunger began to growl in their stomachs. Again one of the witches snapped her fingers and another clapped and movement and speech returned to Srani.

They ordered her to bake them some bread, for bread is the sign of life and bread made for a witch will give her a hold in that household. But they wanted to torment her too, for that is the way of some of the witches of Slievenamon. One by one, they spat upon the flames of the fire, making it grow dimmer and weaker. Despite her terror, Srani bristled at their gall, knowing they were making her task harder while seeking to claim residence in her home through the eating of bread. Worried for her children and husband, Srani turned to her kitchen to gather up the ingredients. She saw that the only water she had was that which she had used to wash her young children's feet earlier that evening and forgotten to dispose of before nightfall. Water used to wash children's feet had the power to grant entry to malevolent forces, as those little feet are wont to wander unknowingly into perilous places. She moved to pick up the bucket, to go and get fresh water, but the witches all hissed and shrieked at her, shouting at her not to touch the feet-water but to take the sieve to the local well. They cackled as her understanding of the impossible task sank in, thinking to themselves it would keep her occupied as they burrowed deeper into their work.

Srani was fearful of leaving her sleeping family alone in the house but, petrified and with little other choice, she calmed herself and went to the well. As expected, each scoop of water in the sieve lasted only seconds before all had drained away into either the well or after a few steps on the path towards her family. Panic began to come over Srani as she could not return without the water. Soon her own face was wet with the weeping of tears. As desperation grew within her, a soft, calm voice arose out of the well, telling her to gather some of the clay about the well and the moss that grew upon it and to mix them, for they would plug the holes of the sieve.

Srani acted quickly and soon she had a vessel that could carry the water. She rushed home and was relieved to see that her husband and children were still sleeping, unharmed. She went to check on them, holding her sieve of water, shaking the beds with her foot to try to raise them from their slumber, but they remained deep in the grasp of sleep. Her relief soon turned again to distress as she realised that they too were under the enchantment of the twelve witches and could not and would not be woken.

Srani began to make the bread for the witches and plot a plan to get rid of the unwelcome visitors. She remembered the tales and rumours of the witches who had made their home at the top of the mountain. As soon as the bread had risen on the fire, she went to the window and let out a great scream: 'Look! Look! There is fire in the sky and the mountain is aflame!'

The witches rose up in fright and took flight to the mountaintop of Slievenamon to save their dwelling place. Knowing that they would soon return, Srani began to undo their enchantments and return her home to its own order.

First she took some bread, broke it and touched it to the lips of her sleeping children and husband, before tossing it upon the fire, which leaped out in great flames as the bread burned. As the smoke rose so did her family from their beds. Next she took the feet-water and sprinkled it around her home and garden, dispersing its power and blocking entry for the witches. Then she took one of the sky-blue cords that the witches had left, knotted it to turn the witches' magic against them, and placed it above her door.

Sooner than expected the witches returned and began to kick and scratch and knock upon the door. This time Srani knew not to open it. The witches grew angry and began to scream at the windows and howl down the chimney, demanding to be allowed entry.

One called out, 'Open! Open! Feet-water! Open!' but the feet-water could not aid the witches, for it was sprinkled and was making its way back to the river.

Another called out, 'Open! Open! Bread! Open!' but the bread could give no help for it was broken and burned upon the fire.

Another then called out, loud and shrill, 'Open! Open! Door of this home, made from wood from our forest! Open!' But the door could give no entry for it was enchanted by the cord and had no power to move.

The witches had been bested and the fear once felt by Srani rose up in the witches. They gasped frantically and gazed about themselves waiting for the wind that would whip them high up into the air. A storm formed as quick as an intake of breath and they were flown up and back like crumpled leaves caught in a sudden gust. Srani could see their faces aflame with anger, eyes bulging and legs kicking, crying out in sharp curses to her until they grew smaller and smaller, their voices fainter and weaker upon the horizon until eventually they were out of sight.

Srani took to the markets the very next day and sold each blanket, cord, skein and roving, and made more than a pretty penny. Never again would she see any of the twelve witches of the horns.

S
P
I
D
E
O
G

Samhain is our month of the holy souls, the saints and the forgotten, a time when we visit the resting places of loved ones. We eat again their foods, play their favourite songs to remind them and ourselves that they still accompany us on our journeys, that they remain alive in and with us. I can't recall who first told me this tale, but it's one I often retell myself as the darker nights of Samhain approach. This story, like many stories of the robin, rests on the edge of the minds of those who keep the tradition of the spideog as wayfinder and soul-talker alive. Children will be encouraged to search for her, the queen of birds, at funerals, a kind way to distract them and a source of comfort to all. She is often seen near the anniversaries of passed loved ones, a garden visitor who brings to mind the dear and the departed.

The sun was slowly setting in the Inagh Valley, in the western lands of the Irish isle, and as the light descended, the shadows stretched and gave a great reach across the lands, claiming them back from the brightness of day to the dimmer fields of night.

An old woman moved through the grounds on her journey home. She was wrapped in a heavy shawl, patterned and patched with echoes of once-vibrant colours, the mossy green of the forest floor, red like flame, and the yellow of a May eve blossom. She was tall and thin-limbed with an age-swept face. Her hair, once ochre, still held streaks of reddish brown in the ashy grey. She moved slowly but with great care, as if not to crush blossom or bush beneath her feet. Her breath was strained and she wheezed with effort and ache. As the sun began to touch the horizon and the light diminished, her progress became even more laboured. Once night had made itself known, the old woman dropped down wearily and rested her head on a bunching of her cloak. She made long, deep, sorrowful wails, stifling them by holding the bundled material to her mouth. Grief was heavy upon her and so deep that it made stale the very air about her. Out of respect, the flowers of the valley, who knew her well, rarely blossomed in her presence. The leaves would resist rustling upon the branches and the birds of the sky neither chirped nor gave swift flutter to their wings when in sight of her. Except for one.

The robin of the valley, though small, was swift and fierce. Her red chest was louder than her voice and announced her inner fire. The warm amber colours of her breast marked both the tenacity of her heart and the bravery of her spirit, maintaining her brightness in even the darkest of places.

The old woman, bound up in her grief, did not at first see the robin when it glided down and took, with nimble feet, a seat beside her. The robin regarded the old woman with a soft tilt of her head, wondering what had befallen her. The bird remained sitting there with the weeping woman, just to be near her. After some time the old woman noticed the robin, and as she gazed upon the little bird, her heart's pain began to unspool itself and out of her mouth poured all of her life, the misery of losing those she loved, the agony she had endured and the malady of living in a world in which she felt so very alone. She spoke of her youth, those days of dreaming when life paths were forged. She told of a great love she had encountered and, with careless thought, had lost. They were to be reunited later, in the bright brass days of their lives, but she had once again lost him, this time not to carelessness or dispute, but to a more unbending foe – death.

The stories kept flowing from the old woman, of the first kiss and the last embrace, of the secrets they had shared huddled by the fires, of the evenings and afternoons spent soaking their feet at the riverside. She even told of how he overfilled his tobacco pipe in the mornings, making plumes of smoke that would rise like soft ashen clouds just above his head. She spoke too of his smile and laughter, of their shared humour. As she spoke, she turned a ring upon her finger, the smith-made promise of a wedding planned but never fulfilled. In their excitement with each other, they chose to run away into the time that they had left together, and those days were filled with so much joy and connection that they both thought they would outlive the bitterness of loss. Still, they both wore a ring, a promise to keep a promise. But a promise is no bar to the hungry hands of time, and her lover was taken. The wound of their sundering was such a mark upon her that nature's colours were dull to her, the sounds of the world around her were dim and distant, and her home felt like it was forever behind her.

The robin listened to every word the old woman spoke, drinking in every memory. She felt the old woman's loss keenly and fluttered to the cradle of her collarbone, expanding a wing to wipe a tear away.

The robin was a creature of the wild and could reach all corners of the world, the places unseen by human eyes. She decided she would search out the lost love. Although she didn't know where to find the answers, she took flight.

The robin went first to the graveyard and found no answers. Next she flew to the barren lands of the great famines and found them empty of aid. Next she flew to the highest mountaintops to speak with those who loved to journey, and from there to the ships on the seas to question the water wayfarers, but they had no insight. She was near to surrendering, as lost as the old woman herself. She took a rest upon the branches of a great oak tree and paced in frustration. As she paced, she shook the annoyance from her head. Then she heard a group of people speaking beneath the tree. They spoke of Tigh Doinn, on an island in the west, a home that once brought shelter to the living but now was a comfort to the dead.

Finally, an answer.

The journey to the island was a dangerous one as the winds stood guard over it and the waters about it were rough and ice cold, colder than the last breaths of those who gathered on the island. The fierce waves hurled water high up into the sky like slivers of blades against all those who would approach. With brawn and conviction the robin flew against the howls of the winds and the strikes of the water to finally make it to land. As the robin flew above the island, she saw what she was looking for. There at the northern edge of the island was a small hut made from dolmen stone, with worn hides draped over it, sewn together with frayed twine by rough hands. It looked like neither the grave it was nor the home it could have been.

The brave robin approached the house and grave. She knew it was a strange place; the two buildings were melded into one and neither was at peace with the other. She flew in between a gap, between the stone and hide and found to her surprise that it was empty. She explored the tight space. It was infused with low light and the scent of mould, and another odour, stale and rotten, hung thick in the air. She heard a thrumming echoing out of the ground, as if the earth itself was beating a drum. As she listened, voices emerged, the aching croaks of another world, low groans mingled with a higher pitch like the sound of a blunt blade thrashing upon a stone.

The robin began to peck at the earth and to use the tips of her small, strong feet to craw against the soil, disturbing the long-dead roots and entangled rot, casting aside the few worms it had to offer, making sure not to eat with the dead. Eventually the ground gave way in a pocket-sized hole, and a faint underworldly glow curled up from beneath. It moved like an uncoiling hand whose fist had spread wide, rising up with a beckoning finger to welcome her down.

And down she went.

She entered a vast hall, with pillars and arches that stretched wide and deep, set at their base with large granite blocks. While tired from her search, from the journey to the island and the digging, she still had within her the strength of swift flight. Flying in ever-increasing circles, she could not find where the walls and rows of monstrous columns ended.

She became aware that the air was shimmering with faint shapes, as cobwebs tremble in a still room. All around were the eerie creaks of sun-bleached bones as they were stood upon, crackling and fracturing, sharply toned but dulled by the distance. In time the robin realised that what she was seeing was the guise and form of the dead, those who had once walked above and now wander below. Their faces were sullied and ingrained with indifference; their skin, rough and crumpled, gleamed with a moisture of unwitnessed rain damp like the earth deep underground. Where there were once ears there were little knolls, as on a tree where a branch has been severed. Where there were once mouths there was no more than a stretch of the skin, as if the jaws had shut and warped, the flesh like a melted pool of a beeswax. Above their cheeks, where there should have been eyes, there was nothing but flat pits of black and maudy brown. There were some there too who were more intact, a dimmed and darkened mirror of their living form, the ones, perhaps, who were still remembered above the ground and so remembered themselves enough to take shape.

The robin, in her wisdom, knew not to gaze too long at the holes where eyes had once moved and danced with life, for fear that her long gaze would capture death's attention. As she approached, most of those in the great hall ignored her, neither casting a glance nor moving. She knew to limit her time with the dead, for should she stay too long, they would claim her unlived days ahead. So she took again to her task to find the lost lover of the old woman of the valley. Not knowing his name, she sang out his story, of the life lived and the love lost, of secret hopes shared in the embrace of the valley and how, in the desperation of pain, a woman's life had been stilled and all of its potential soured.

Eventually the robin grew tired and, not wanting to perch upon the shoulders of any of the dead for fear they would grasp and hold her within that world, she rested on the ground of the great hall, before making her mind clear that she would leave and return, without victory, to the valley. Just as she was about to take flight, she noticed on the hand of one of the dead a smith-made ring, just like the ring the old woman wore. Taking a chance, the robin approached the figure and sung again the story of the lovers. On recognising his tale, the man turned to the robin. His darksome presence became lighter, his form became more clearly drawn, and the robin could see his handsome features.

The dead in truth rarely speak, because most have no breath, though some hold on to the very edges of their last sigh. Moved by memories, the dead man leaned forward and spoke a secret to the robin in a low mumbling groan.

The robin gleefully took the whisper from the spectre and tucked it tight under one of her wings and took flight from the great hall and the barren island. This time, however, the waters were calm, as if accepting of her travel. The wind which once fought her back now moved with smooth blow upon her, speeding her along.

On her return to the valley, the robin found the woman sitting as she had left her, but weaker and fainter now, for all her tears had been cried and her body was as dry and fragile as light kindling. No sooner had the robin approached the old woman than she dropped the heavy cloth of her cloak, which had become even more ragged from the tight curling fingers that in grief and sorrow had torn at the fabric.

The woman recognised that the robin did not approach her the same way as before; this time the robin had brought something back, a whisper from her departed lover, and while her ears could not hear the utterance, her heart most certainly did. On recognising the gift, she began to shake off the cold slumber and regain some warmth and, while the message did not take the pain of loss from her, it eased the heaviness that clung to her heart.

Word of the kindness of the robin spread within the valley. Requests came to the robin from all those who had the company of grief to carry words to their dead, so that perhaps they too would have the blessing of a lost loved one in return. Within a season the robin was guiding more of her kin to the island, each with a tale of the living to trade for a heart's reply.

With such frequent visits and the sharing of songs, the dead grew less cold, warmed by the visits of those who traded cares and comments between the dead and the bereft, ferrying hopes and connections from one world to another, forging a path where heartfelt tears alone could not.

In the halls of the dead, in the deep grounds beneath the home of the lost, being remembered holds a truly transformative power. To be forgotten is a forever death. For this reason and many more, the robin is held in high regard. In time, those who lived in the valley decided that if a wren could be a king of the birds for wit and cunning, then a robin could be more than a queen for strength, grace and kindness. To this day the robin still brings the messages from the dead and listens to any open heart that is willing to speak.

The winter solstice marks the end of the long nights and welcomes in the glow of the newborn sun. A time of celebration and release of worry, knowing that the bright days of spring will soon arrive. This retelling is about how a fein shaped the very edges of the winter season and has long been cherished for it, overlooking that before him this burden had been carried by a woman. I've always understood this story to be about the consistent and unnoticed work and responsibility that women are expected to undertake and do accomplish. The weight of the unacknowledged terrible pressure that can either break many women or force them to diverge from their chosen path. I was in primary school when I read about the trials of Hercules and his near-impossible tasks. I realised the shared depth in both tales. Hercules was celebrated for great feats and undertakings that were largely made possible by unnamed women.

Who first told me this tale remains beyond my recall, although I think it was a woman, as the hints of her laughter are at the edges of my memory. I think it may have been an aunt, but I cannot in truth put a name to the story with any certainty, which sadly seems to be in line with many of the stories told over time by women, who become mostly anonymous. I share this not only as an act of remedy but as a thank you for a gift so freely given.

Nature has its own rhythm, moving at its own pace and dancing into the days and nights with little regard to the clock upon the wall or the calendars that chart the days.

It is said, though, that the seasons were untamed in the past. A summer could last a day and the autumn could stretch for what might seem a lifetime; spring could descend and pass as swiftly as a cycle of the moon; and winter, winter was a visitor who never knew when to leave. And this is how it was for generations untold.

That was of course until a man called Stofirt met a goddess called the Cailleach. Stofirt was short and slender, with boots of thick, worn leather. By his side he carried a staff of oak with grains and knots. Like a second skin, he wore a shawl of waxed yellow linen with frayed edges, pulled tight across his body. His long hair was flinty grey and held flickers of rust like sparks in the night. His clothes were tied with a crios of rowan red and old copper green. Stofirt had a youthful mischief about him, which shone brightly from his cheerful smile, yet he was made sombre by his firm brow that framed his darting eyes, keen to see what might be concealed and swift to catch sight of fluttering birds' wings.

Winter had come and stayed so long that young boys grew long, grey, knotted beards and the youthful maidens of the homestead had more grandchildren than they could count upon their fingers and toes. So long was the visit that the larders grew bare and the land ached for growth and the warmth of a brighter sun. The kindred of the sky were among the last things left to eat, for those who could sleep the winter soundly slept and the grain seeds rarely sprouted. It had been many years since the fish of the rivers and lakes had risen to the surface, with the waves rarely breaking away from winter's dense icy grasp.

The word was known among the people that the winter was held in place by a woman. Some said she was a sage of the wild, others that she was the goddess of the people of the high mountains who came before memories of the land were kept, before the first song was sung and before the naming of the berries of the brambles.

Stofirt, having grown up in a world of near-barren larders and of nights that stretched out in the dark bleakness and the shrill cold that bit the very marrow of his bones, longed for days of warmth and evenings with no terror of a hearth empty of firewood. He wished for days in which he could cross the field barefoot and smell fresh, sweet pollen as it moved between the trees. He yearned for rising dawns that would wake the sleeping butterflies and sunsets like scarlet bonfires on the horizon. Instead, the sun was a meagrely fed candle, burning dimly on a faraway cliff.

One morning Stofirt decided to go in search of the woman who kept winter, and began to visit each mountain in Ireland in hope that their paths would cross. He would plead with her to draw back the gales of snow and give way to a new and fresher time, the springtime he had never witnessed but had always longed for.

On a darksome evening as Stofirt crossed the lands of Loughcrew, he finally came across the Cailleach he had so long and longingly searched for. She was old and tall, noble, with strong shoulders braced high on a back that was twisted slightly from age. Like the yews of the forest she had known time, and time had known her. Her skin was sun-touched and frost-worn, with wrinkles deep like folds of fabric. Her hair was grey like the stones of the Burren, woven in a loose plait, wisps dancing with the wind and stretching like webs across her forehead. She wore a thick woollen cloak that draped over her body like the wilting willow boughs. The cloak had a high-peaked hood, which she used to shield her face from the elements and ensure her warmth. She kept thunder in the soles of her feet, snow and sleet in her pockets and the mightiest of gales she kept bound up in a silver comb tucked into the top of her plait. She was known for visiting the mountaintops, jumping from one to another when the mood caught her, which it regularly did, especially if a visitor stayed beyond the Cailleach's brief welcome.

Her eyes, the dark brown of fresh stirred earth, fixed upon Stofirt as he approached her, narrowing slightly with each step he took, both irascible and curious about who had come to disturb her. With each pace, his thick leather boots began to feel more like thin silk, his feet shaking, no longer firm upon the snowy ground. He stood before the Cailleach, holding up to the sky the symbol of his own god, shaped with two sprigs of wood, and commanded that she withdraw the winter.

The Cailleach rolled her eyes to the grey clouds that hung heavy above them and ignored Stofirt, turning to make her journey from him. She had no notion of returning to the great toil of withdrawing winter year in and year out. Stofirt, not to be deterred, quickly took to a geiging that would make the golden honey look as pale as time-worn tin. He asked the Cailleach to claim back the ice and frost, but again she simply flicked her hand to dismiss his pleas.

With his request dismissed and his words of charm having found no home in her ears, Stofirt dropped to his knees and held the hem of her robes in desperation. His heart poured out every want he had, not only for the winter to end but every secret wish from the corners of his soul and the edges of his mind. The Cailleach was taken aback by his honesty and openness. Although she had looked at him before, this was the first time she had seen him and her interest was piqued. He wanted something from her, but now she could see that she might have a need for him, if he could prove his mettle. Firmly but with a quick graceful turn, she took her robe from his grip and raised her hands like two bowls to catch the drizzle of rain as it fell. She made no chant, she mimicked no trance, there was no dancing and no mumbling of arcane words. Just stillness and silence but for the dripping rain.

After some time, she moved closer to Stofirt, resting both hands upon his shoulders and aiding him to his feet. She asked him if he could make for her a broom so that she could sweep away the snowfall and the deep bite of winter. Joy danced in the heart of Stofirt and loudly he exclaimed 'Yes!' as his body rushed with the swell of happiness, making him warmer than he had felt in all the years of his life.

The Cailleach took from Stofirt his oak walking staff, commenting on how old and strong it was, having carried him on his journey for some time, and how it would aid him in his quest. She told him to go gather hazel from the highest point at which it grows upon the isle of Ireland so that she could make her broom. Quicker than the flexed paws of wolves, Stofirt was on his way to Carrauntoohil.

Having reached the peak of the mountain, he slowly made his way down its treacherous slopes until he saw, growing against a small stone wall, the twisted form of a hazel tree. Stofirt took his time taking branches from the tree. The deep frost made it as strong as steel and sharp like glass so that he shredded the skin of his fingers. He paid no heed to the spatters of blood on the snow that lay about the roots of the hazel tree; his will was firm that he would return with the wood. As soon as he had all the branches, he gathered them up, holding them tight against his chest with his forearms so as to protect his wounded hands. He returned to the Cailleach and gleefully presented the branches to her. She picked them up and examined them, frowned and turned to Stofirt, then asked for more branches. This time he was to leave her side and travel to the lowest lands of Ireland and return with him all the alder he could carry.

His heart grew heavy that the hazel was not enough but he would not be swayed from his undertaking. Stofirt again left the Cailleach and travelled to the south-east of the island, to the lands of Slob. He waded his way deep into the icy waters to reach the lowest point and from there climbed out and up to higher lands in search of the alder. No sooner had he left the waters than there on the horizon stood an alder tree moving slowly in the chilled air, like an old friend waving a greeting.

On approaching the tree, he realised that his hands were too damaged to break off the twigs. Instead he held the branches between his arms and snapped them off one by one. The frozen limbs of the alder, like shards of jet, cut and tore at him, gashing wounds deep into his chest and arms. Still he persevered. When he had all he could carry of the alder, Stofirt balanced his offering upon his shoulders and travelled back to the Cailleach.

On returning to her camp, Stofirt realised that the pile of hazel wood he had left had greatly shrunk and he called out to the Cailleach, asking what had happened. She replied that while waiting for him she grew cold and took to burning some of the wood in her fire. Upon examining the alder, the Cailleach rocked her head, accepting the wood, and told Stofirt what a good job he had done. But in the keeping of the fire there was simply not enough to make the broom. For his wish to be granted, he would need to return to the road and bring back some holly from a tree that grew near the cave of Oweynagat, the cave of the cats.

Sighing loudly, but fixed on his goal, Stofirt took to the winding roads of Ireland again and travelled to Oweynagat. He rested beside the cave's entrance and there, growing at the mouth of the cave and entangled along the hedge line, was holly growing in scattered heaps. Knowing the state of his hands from the hazel and the wounds on his arms and chest from the alder, he decided he would snap the branches off the holly with his shoulders and back. With sharp turns and jolts he knocked many of the twigs from the bush, and they snagged on his linen cloak. The holly was blade-like from the long winter's breath, and many of the briars tore deep into his flesh and shredded his cloak. Wearier now than ever before, his hands raw, his arms bloodied and his shoulders and back pierced, Stofirt had to tie the holly to his thick leather boots with his crios, and he moved as quick as he could to the molly, to bring the holly to the Cailleach.

When he arrived, he saw the branches of hazel and alder still stacked high, but much diminished. He cried out to the Cailleach who was warming her hands by the fire. Realising she had once again taken the wood to keep the fire, he kicked the holly up on top of the woodpile with a loud sigh. On approaching the pile, the Cailleach hummed and hawed, measured for herself the wood and checked the strength of each branch. When she spoke again to Stofirt, she said that it was not yet enough for her to sweep away all the snow and sleet from the land, and that if he could withstand the weather once more, would he once again find some more for her?

Stofirt sighed heavily, and with tears welling in his eyes and a voice that was about to crack as sharply as the wood that he had carried, accepted again the task to find more. This time the Cailleach asked him to travel to Legnashinna, the watery source pot of the River Shannon, and bring home to her some crab-apple branches.

It took days and nights for Stofirt to find his way to the Shannon pot, and having again taken some rest from his journey, he found a crab-apple tree standing strong and firm just within eyeshot of the frozen waters. This time, having grown so tired of his travel, Stofirt was greatly worried about how he would take the wood. His hands were cut, his arms and chest wounded, his back was bruised and torn. He decided that he would use his feet and kick every branch he could reach from the tree.

Although the cold had burrowed deeply into his flesh and the dampness of sorrow had mouldered his mind, he gathered up a bundle of twigs. Like all the other trees, the crab apple had grown sharp with the cold. But it had also become rugged with age, and as some crab apples do, it had grown spiteful and bitter. While his thick leather boots at first provided some protection, with each kick of the tree the seams stretched and their stitches snapped, until they only stayed on his feet because the leather had moulded to their shape. Stomping and driving his feet into the crab-apple tree had taken its toll. His feet were mangled, and he had deep blue bruises from the tips of his toes to his knees. Stofirt's feet and legs looked as if they had been dipped in a well of livid ink, like the quills of the monks. Not to be broken, Stofirt rose to his feet, although barely able to stand, and this time held what branches he could between his teeth and carried them back to the camp of the Cailleach.

On his return his head and heart dropped when he saw the wood pile was again shrunken. He approached the Cailleach, crying out that he felt tormented and harmed by her. When the old woman rose to her feet, in response to his claim a roll of thunder crossed the air between them. Stofirt immediately grew quiet and fearful of her. The Cailleach turned towards the woodpile, saying that there was nearly enough wood, but not quite enough for her to make the besom that would sweep away the hailstones. And she asked, if he was not yet broken by it all, if he would he go to the graveside of the great plague and bring to her some whitethorn.

While bone-weary and bed-wanting, bruised, cut, wounded and limping, Stofirt took again to the road and, as soon as he had landed his eye on the soil of Tallaght, found a whitethorn growing along a roadside. With fingers torn and arms cut, with back bruised and scratched, with a deep grinding pain in his feet, he decided he would again use his teeth to rip as many branches as he could from the tree. Gnawing and tearing, he slowly cut the branches from the tree, which was as strong as pyrite and fractured into slivers, cutting his lips and gums, and he lost tooth after tooth to the bark. After much effort and great pain, Stofirt had before him a meagre bundle of sprigs and no idea how he would ever be able to take them back the Cailleach. All he could do was lie beside the twigs and cry.

A deep sorrow flowed from him and soon his heart was made

smoother from the release of his pain. Having decided to give up, he stood on shaking legs and found that some of his hair was tangled among the twigs of the whitethorn tree, and he thought that perhaps this was a way to take them to the Cailleach. Tossing his head back and forth, he caught most of the twigs and again, weary but still unbested, he took to the roads, back to she who was tending the fire.

On his arrival, not wanting to look upon the woodpile, he approached the old woman and asked would this be enough for the broom. She sat him down and slowly untangled each sprig from his hair, measuring and weighing them in her hands and checking the shape of them with her exacting eyes, and, after offering Stofirt some tea from her own cup, she spoke words sharper to him than any of the branches. 'Not yet,' she said. To finish the broom, he would need to find a rath that belonged to the Good People and take for her some rowan, the mountain ash.

Stofirt was almost broken but managed to again gather his senses and went in a search of the mountain ash. He had not travelled far before finding a rath and resting against it for some time to catch his breath and gather his strength. By now his hands were bloody, his arms scored, his back slashed, feet twisted and teeth crushed. All he had left was his hair, which he unbraided and threw high into the air until it became tangled amongst the branches of the mountain ash. He rested his aching body against the tree while his hair frosted over and stuck to a branch. Then he swung, using his hair as a rope, until his weight and perseverance broke the branch, taking down a bundle of twigs.

Rising again to his feet, with as much strength as he could muster, he took to the road that led back to the old woman, with the twigs dangling behind him. The journey was as rough as all those before, but this time he was not sure if he would make it. The twigs behind him scratched against the road as he walked, snapping much of his frozen hair as he made his way. As soon as he had stepped inside the camp of the Cailleach, the last strand of his hair broke and the branch fell firmly to the ground next to the woodpile. Stofirt again resisted taking a full look at the pile, not having the heart in him to check if it had fared better than before.

This time the old woman beckoned to him and sat him by the fire, giving him once again her cup to drink from and this time also her bowl to eat from. As Stofirt shivered, the woman took a corner of her cloak and wrapped it around him, bringing great comfort and peace to his body as well as his mind. Having taken some rest and restoration from the tea, food and warmth of the cloak, Stofirt nervously looked at the Cailleach and asked her in a hoarse, tired voice if there was now enough wood to make the broom.

She turned to him and drew out from under the edge of her cloak a single blade, formed from bone and sharply pointed, and whispered to him, 'Almost.' She curled her finger to welcome him closer and then pointed to a tree at the edge of the field, and said, 'Take for me a branch of birch from this field that I have made my home, and I will make for you the broom that will sweep away snow and frost, hail and gale and storm, thunder and the gloom of dark skies. If you,' continued the Cailleach, 'get for me even a single branch from the tree, I will make it for you.'

Stofirt had as little breath left as he did strength and will. He was so weak he could only crawl out from under the cloak of the Cailleach. As he struggled, a fresh thought passed through his mind. He would trick her into cutting her own wood and in that way bring the endless trial to an end. A clever thought indeed, and with this secret idea hidden away in the wink of his eye, he refused the blade, but made his way towards the tree.

While the tree did not look far away, the land seemed to stretch and grow as he moved towards it. An inch felt like a foot, and the foot a length of several miles. Still, he crawled on until at last he reached it, and with a last flicker of will, he rose to his feet. Working through pain and loss, he called out insults to the Cailleach to raise her ire. He mocked her, claiming she had stolen the heat of the fire, never having gathered any wood herself. The sound of his words ignited such fury in her that her very breaths grew hot and made the frosty air mild. She turned and threw her blade at him. As it sped swiftly through the air, Stofirt quickly threw himself to the ground. The knife grazed his tattered shawl and hit the birch tree, cleaving from it a full branch with many twigs. As he lay beside the fallen wood, he placed his hand upon it and called out again to the Cailleach in such soft tones that the wind threatened to take the words away before they were heard: 'Now you've gathered your own wood.'

As understanding of his clever trick dawned on the old woman, the coal left the fire of her anger and the sternness left her face, replaced by a quick smile. Chuckling at his cunning, the old woman approached the fallen man and tenderly picked him up as if he was but a bundle of duck feathers. With the branches gathered up beneath her other arm, she took Stofirt and the wood to the fireside and began to make the broom. Using the oak as a staff, she gathered in the hazel and the alder, the holly and the crab apple, the whitethorn, rowan and mountain ash. Finally, she placed some of the birch on the staff. She tied the broom with some of Stofirt's hair, which had been warmed and untangled by the heat of her fire to make the broom twigs hold firm and fast.

Stofirt, bald and broken, toothless and bruised, watched the

Cailleach and she returned his gaze with a soft admiration. She placed a single kiss upon his forehead. As soon as her lips touched his brow, Stofirt was enveloped in a bright glow, which he quickly realised was that of fresh sunlight, unhampered by the thick dreary clouds that had long hung in the sky. As the light streamed down and Stofirt bathed in its comfort, like a newborn lamb against the warmth of its mother's body, he began to recover. His hands, once cut, began to heal as if a fresh balm was covering them. The wounds on his arms and chest began to knit together as if they were being sewn by unseen hands. His back, curled in pain, began to unfurl itself from the grip of agony, and his toes and feet began to return to how they once were. He reached for his mouth and found his teeth restored and his gums intact. Suddenly his hair fell in front of his eyes, as if dropped by some bird. It too was restored.

As Stofirt lay there in wonder at his recovery, the Cailleach was busy finishing the broom, and finally it was made. The Cailleach took the handle and breathed in deeply in giddy anticipation. A smile grew across Stofirt's lips. He who had travelled so far and trialled so much was brimming with excitement to see the Cailleach finally brush away the winter. To his surprise, she tossed the broom to him to make the sweep. And sweep he did. With his body no longer worn and tired, Stofirt gripped the oak with vigour. With every touch of the broom, the ice and snow turned to water, warm and lively. The pale hands of winter withdrew as Stofirt travelled the lands, making green where once there was grey, breaking soil for the long-sleeping seeds, melting the frozen waters for salmon to splash, and ensuring that the colour blue was no longer a stranger to the sky above all those who lived on the island. For most, this was the first ever sight of spring.

The Cailleach was delighted. The burden was no longer on her and nature would return to its natural rhythm. Long had she carried the labour of winter's keep unaided. As aeons passed, she had grown weary of such responsibility, but her noble spirit ensured that she would not abandon the duty but rather find a new caretaker, testing their mettle by her fire. Stofirt had proved both his strength and his wit, the new custodian of the Cailleach's besom and the steward of the season of winter. Since that day and every year since, Stofirt crosses the land of Ireland, sweeping as he goes, ensuring that the snow of winter recedes and that the seasons run forever forward.

ACKNOWLEDGEMENTS

A sincere thank you to Nidhi, Fionnuala and Gráinne of Skein Press, a publishing home that heard my voice and wanted to share it. You remain a heart's delight to me. Thanks too to Mahito and Chandrika in Skein, to Cormac for publicity and to Robert for proofreading.

Thank you to the Tyrone Guthrie Centre, for the space and grace of a good view, a welcoming table and the kindness of newfound friends.

Heartfelt gratitude to Deirdre and Yingge for your sharing, caring and the forge-hot bright sparks of inspiration. We journeyed wide and found unsung songs amongst each other. Thank you, Éilís, for blessing us with your craft.

Mo gris mo grath, Dan, 'Himself', and the wiggly-tailed Chester; you see me.